TOMORROW'S SON

Also by Robert Hoskins

Novels

THE SHATTERED PEOPLE
MASTER OF THE STARS
TO CONTROL THE STARS

Anthologies

FIRST STEP OUTWARD
INFINITY ONE
THE STARS AROUND US
SWORDS AGAINST TOMORROW
INFINITY TWO
TOMORROW 1
THE FAR-OUT PEOPLE
INFINITY THREE
· WONDERMAKERS
STRANGE TOMORROWS
INFINITY FOUR
INFINITY FIVE
THE EDGE OF NEVER
WONDERMAKERS 2
THE LIBERATED FUTURE
SAVING TOMORROW

TOMORROW'S SON

ROBERT HOSKINS

DOUBLEDAY & COMPANY, INC.

GARDEN CITY, NEW YORK 1977

All of the characters in this book
are fictitious, and any resemblance
to actual persons, living or dead,
is purely coincidental.

Library of Congress Cataloging in Publication Data

Hoskins, Robert.
Tomorrow's son.

I. Title.
PZ4.H828Tom   [PS3558.076]   813'.5'4
ISBN: 0-385-12100-8
Library of Congress Catalog Card Number 76-2782

This one is for Ann . . .

1970460

TOMORROW'S SON

ONE

The dark moon rose over the eastern horizon, its disc a barely seen pale red in the last afternoon rays of the sun. Dusk was slipping over the ancient city's towers, the narrow twisting streets already in night darkness beneath the overhanging upper stories of the tenement district.

There were few lights in the latter area, although an occasional flickering torch marked the door to a public house. An upper window opened briefly, emitting a wan orange glow as a pot of garbage was emptied into the broad gutter that ran through the center of the street.

Cursing, Clay Holland jumped back from the sudden splat of refuse, but not in time. He drew out a linen handkerchief and tried to scrub away the more visible spots on his robe, then crumpled the square of cloth and tossed it into the gutter. Its whiteness seemed out of place as it floated on top of the scum.

"Watch your footing!" said his companion.

Clay brought his attention back to the present in time to step over the decaying corpse of a small animal. It seemed similar to a Terran dog, despite a rough skin that resembled blue scales.

"Ahhhhhh!" Again he sidestepped to avoid a pile of ordure, and wiped the back of his hand across his insulted nose. "Does everything here stink?"

"That it does," his companion said, amiably.

"Including the people," said Clay, fending off a stout fellow who stank of sour beer.

Holland was a tall youth, slenderer than most of the passing natives, and half a head taller. His hair, a natural brown, had been bleached almost white, his complexion ruddied to a deep burnt orange that made him seem a native despite his height. Drab pilgrim's robes masked the unusual straightness of his stance while a heavy cowl drooped low over his eyes, hiding his expression.

"You do grow used to it in time," said his guide. "After a long time."

He was a shorter, stouter version of Holland, except that his robe was the bleached homespun of a priest. From time to time a native brushed against him in the shadows; one started to mutter an apology—breaking off in a snarl as his robes were recognized.

"*Damn!*" The curse came from a native, who wiped foulness from his robes and shouted upward imprecations without pausing in his journey. The one above who had dumped the chamber pot screamed back shrill invective before slamming the window.

"I thought sanitation rated an A priority," said Clay.

Martin, the other agent, shrugged. "Earth policy and field practice frequently have little in common, Holland. Forget what they taught you back at Academy—lesson number one in field service."

"Still, for our own benefit . . ."

"It would be nice, yes, but impractical. Too many dreamers back on Earth have the power to assign priority classifications. Once you are on the client planet you learn that many of the niceties can wait until Contact Day—if it ever comes."

He seemed suddenly bitter. Clay tried to make out his features in the gloom.

"I thought the date for Karyllia was already targeted," said the youth.

"Oh, it is." The older man sounded weary. "Don't mind me, Holland—field fatigue is getting to me. I've had the charades, the games. I'd rather be working in the open, honestly, than skulking about in the robes of this phony religion."

"The cultural shock would be too great."

"You're citing the training log," said Martin. "And so the psychometricians claim. Many of us disagree."

"Why?"

"We've lived Karyllia, Holland. We know the people, their politics, their thought processes. Oh, we know policy—but unfortunately policy doesn't know this planet. If only the ivory tower minds could come out from Earth and work in the field for a while they'd understand the real problems we face trying to drag this stone age culture up by its boot straps."

Clay Holland fell silent, disturbed by the older agent's words. The youth was fresh from Academy, about to start his first assignment away from Earth—and for years he had been anticipating this day.

Conditioned by fifteen years of close-directed education to being an agent, he had been selected five years ago for training as a field operative. Now he was joining the proud vanguard of Earthmen who were working to bring the other two so far discovered hominid populated worlds to the point of free partnership with Earth itself. It was a noble task, one acclaimed by poets for centuries.

Unfortunately for the poets, both of the hominid planets, Karyllia and Locane, were culturally severely retarded. Karyllia was the more advanced, but even here technology was just beginning to touch the native cultures. Locane was still on the nomadic hunter level, although agricultural implants were at last gaining a toehold.

Locane and Karyllia had been discovered within a year of each other by probe teams looking for human-suitable planets for colonization. There were few such worlds within the reach of the first star ships, but Earth was once more feeling the pressures of population, after centuries of stability following the Great Famines of the twentieth century. The census was past the two billion mark again, crowded tight in the 40 per cent of the planet's surface that had not been scoured by the Nuclear War.

Star travel could drain off few of Earth's present excess, but the psychological relief was greater than the physical. Let the planet-bound producing classes think there was a place for them to emigrate to, and they more readily accepted the strictures of staying at home.

There was one problem: as Earth society became completely technological, a greater percentage of the population became consumers only, and there was a general drop in intelligence across every level of population. The curves had flattened for a time, and now were dropping again. That was known, however, to a very limited group of leaders.

First contact with the hominid planets had come fifty years ago. Now Karyllia was showing signs that it was ready to begin a cultural leapfrogging that hopefully would last several generations. Already the technological generation had been shortened to half the time of the social generation, and even that was showing signs of compression.

"How much farther?" asked Clay, after bruising his shoulder on an unseen projection at the corner of a house. He envied Martin's apparent ability to see in the dark.

"We're close now," said the other. "Soon."

The answer was not satisfactory, but Clay could do nothing but accept it, rubbing the sore muscle.

To the casual observer from Earth the technology of Karyllia would have seemed almost nonexistent. The industrial revolution was still in the planet's future, although nearer than it would have been without the agents' direction.

Since the age of fifteen Clay Holland had been conditioned to the reality of this planet, but now that he was actually here it was as though the lecture tapes and field exercises had been no more than pale monochromatic copies of the true situation. The tapes could not reproduce the smells, which were the immediate and first impression to attack the senses of the newcomer.

As with most young men, he was anxious to succeed. He knew that of his generation he had been fortunate enough to be selected for the schools of Earth. Few were chosen for higher training, most assigned at a very early age to the status of drone, the consumers rather than the producers.

Clay was luckier than most, for he had parents who were high placed. But the accident of birth assured him only of a hearing. His own potential had saved him from the welfare ranks. During his parents' lifetimes he could feed from their privileges, but if he could not pass muster himself he would eventually be assigned to the drone barracks. After education, the thought of such an existence was frightening even to contemplate.

There was the clash of distant wheels, although this street had no room for wheeled vehicles. The number of natives was growing thicker as well as the two agents approached the center of the city of Ahd-Abbor. Capital of the surrounding district, the city compressed a native population of several hundred thousand and a transient population of perhaps a hundred thousand more into a space with room for no more than a quarter of that number. Squeezed by ancient walls that lined two rivers, the city could expand only to the north. Consequently it had grown upward, new construction planting foundations on the roofs of the old until the weight became too much to bear and a building or an entire district collapsed.

The transient population came to the city from all over the rest of the continent, and from the surrounding offshore islands as well. Ahd-Abbor lay across the natural confluence of continental trade routes, the two rivers joining here after quartering the central plains to blend their waters into the great river Greyat, which continued another two hundred kilometers to the sea.

The city was constructed on the triangle between the rivers' joining, and with such a disparity of cultures to draw upon could not be anything but cosmopolitan. The traders came with the caravans from the west while the sailing masters beat up the river Greyat with cargoes from the morning islands and from the southern shores. Occasionally a strange-hulled ship would come into the harbor, bearing adventurers from the impossibly distant east.

There was a further reason for Ahd-Abbor's importance, however. As the most ancient city on the continent, it was also the home of the central temple for the dominant native religion. Because of that, the capital had been selected by the men from Earth as the site of their own headquarters, disguised as a temple for a new religion created by the agents.

To Holland's eyes the city was a jumbled mass of twisting streets that barely deserved to be called alleys. This close in, toward the central square and the trade citadel that antedated the city walls, the houses towered four and five flimsy stories high. The lower, older sections were built of native fieldstone for the most part, while the upper levels and most of the construction on the point spilling to the north were of the reddish brick wood that covered the lower slopes of a mountain range a hundred kilometers to the north.

It was from those same mountains that the two agents had just come, dropped by shuttle in a secluded valley above the level inhabited by the farmers and herders. The Earthmen's permanent base was in orbit about the planet. They had made their way down out of the range on foot, but once in the foothills were able to join up with a caravan bound for Ahd-Abbor, dak herders, the scrawny men who watched over the staple meat supply of the region.

They crossed the river on a ferry barge, hemmed in with a load of the eructating daks. Now they were drawing close to the central square, the site of the Sanctum, the native temple, and the off-worlders' own Temple of Eternal Light.

The press of natives was increasing, the crowd growing thicker and moving along in more of a hurry. The streets were becoming even narrower as the agents entered the oldest part of the city; now there was barely room for two to pass alongside the gutter. But Martin's priestly robes were usually enough to ensure an easy passage; few of the locals had liking for the alien religion.

Most of the natives sidled aside into a doorway until the agents were past; then one deliberately brushed against Clay, pushing him heavily. Holland grunted—and Martin reached out a darting hand to grab the little man, hauling him in by

the scruff of the neck. The agent slammed the native against
the nearest wall.

"Hold, little one!"

His words were spoken softly, but the tone of command was
unmistakable as he slipped into the guttural dialect of the city.
Until then the Earthmen had been speaking Standard, the off-
world tongue lost as just one more strange polysyllabic jumble
amid the two-score native languages heard normally in the city.

"Holy!" The little man whined in an unpleasant voice. "I've
done nothing!"

"No?" Martin looked at Clay. "I suggest, brother, that you
check the condition of your purse."

Clay fingered his belt, astonished. "It's gone!"

"But not far—eh?"

The agent slammed the native against the wall again, then
quickly frisked his clothing, coming up with the missing purse.
The tie string was cut.

"Have you no respect, little one, for the Chosen of God?"

"Please, Holy! I'm just a poor fisher—"

"And coin metal is the bait."

Martin continued the search, grunting as he came up with
something else. "And I suppose you found this in the gullet
of a recent catch?"

He held up a long black knife, the blade even in darkness
seemingly chipped from obsidian. It had a leather hilt that was
worn almost through in several places, evidence of age and long
use. The agent tested the blade against his thumb and found
the edge as sharp as it appeared.

"Since when do fishermen carry the membership badge of
the Thieves' Guild?"

The little native suddenly twisted from Martin's grasp, but
before he could break free Clay was reaching out to capture
him, his arms wrapping tight about the thief's middle. Then a
sharp kick on the shin brought stars to his eyes, an elbow in the
midriff doubled him over, and the thief was gone, darting into
the crowd.

Clay started after him, but the other agent held him back, shaking his head.

"Let him go."

"To steal again?"

"What's one more thief in a city of thieves? The jails are overcrowded as it is, and the populace overtaxed to pay for the feeding of them. Here."

He tossed over the knife. "You may as well have a souvenir of your formal welcome to Karyllia. The fellow did you a favor, breaking you in early."

Clay slipped the knife into his belt, wondering if the thief had indeed been a man. During the few seconds that his arms had held the native, the curves of the body had seemed more feminine. Yet Martin apparently had noticed nothing during his search.

The agents were moving again toward the central square when the deep tones of a gong came from a near distance. Its reverberations were more felt than heard, and the surrounding houses seemed to erupt natives. The agents stopped as Clay shook his head, numbed by the tones of the gong.

"The Snakes calling the vermin to evening services," said Martin. "Adjust your filters."

He slipped his hand into his robe and came out with a tiny package, removing the plugs inside and inserting them in his ears. Clay felt for his own as Martin adjusted his—and then staggered as the gong sounded again. His hands went to his ears and he shook his head, trying to clear away the false sparks that had begun to dance across his vision.

"What is it?" asked Martin. "Where are your filters?"

Clay fumbled through his robes again.

"I don't know—I had them when we made final check before entering the shuttle, but they're gone now! The thief—"

The gong sounded a third time before he could finish the statement, and he nearly lost his balance under the force of the blow. The owner of the shop behind them came bursting out in a cloud of flour dust, a rotund little man and the first really fat native the agents had met. He bounced off Clay and disap-

peared around a bend in the narrow street. Few other natives
were in sight now.

Now Clay's face contorted with pain, and Martin grabbed
his arm. "Come on—we'll have to make a run for our temple."

The youth was moving with Martin's urging, but then the
gong sounded its summons for the fourth time. Clay staggered,
isolated muscles starting to convulse in Jacksonian's syndrome,
while his heart seemed about to explode from its chest cavity.

The older agent heaved Clay erect, half supporting him, half
carrying him, as together they staggered into a run. The street
was broadening before them now, better lit by more frequent
torches on the houses. Seconds later they were in the midst of
the trade markets, and then bursting into the great open space
of the central square.

Across the square, sweeping along the entire southern side,
stood the crumbling stone fortress that was the ancient citadel
and that still housed the seat of the city's government. A tribu-
tary of the rivers swept down through the square, the creek
forming a moat along the front of the citadel, a scum- and gar-
bage-filled outlet for the gutter systems of the surrounding
streets.

The opposite compass ends of the square were dominated
equally by the temples of the two important religions—native
and off-world implant. The Earthmen had built their temple to
the west, in a style taken from their own history and completely alien to the planet. The Doric-columned classical structure was built of native basalt blocks that had been bleached
white, and was imposing as it overwhelmed the surrounding native structures. In its position the front of the temple caught
the first rays of the morning sun.

The natives had built to the east, where they could watch
the shadows of evening approaching their Sanctum as the sun
descended toward the horizon. This new religion had been deliberately designed to counteract the night worship of ancient
Karyllia.

Clay saw the Earthmen's temple, which was their destina-
tion, but could spare no energy to look toward the natives'

Sanctum. The square was almost empty of native life now, the two agents the only ones moving toward the west. Everyone else was heeding the call to Darkness.

"Come on, lad! Move!"

Martin tugged at him, the square impossibly huge to Clay's blurring vision as he staggered over its ancient paving blocks. It seemed to be taking them forever to reach their goal, and safety.

Now there was a blare of warning trumpets, unheard earlier in the pulsing subsonics from the great gong. The clarion call was repeated twice as Martin tried to urge the youth into faster movements. Clay was unable to summon the normal reserves of his body, his muscles refusing to answer his demands. He staggered again, fell to his knee.

"You can't stay out here!" said Martin. "You've got to get into the temple!"

"Try'n," said Clay, mumbling. His jaw hung loose, saliva drooling as he let the older agent force him once more to his feet. "He'p me!"

Now they were almost to the temple steps, but the great gong sounded again, impossibly louder than before in the open space of the square. Its tones were more felt than heard, tormenting muscle tissue and bone structure and burning with white pain through the unprotected brain. The filters would have made it bearable, although the muscles would still have felt the pain. But Clay had no protection at all.

The thief: his fading mind focused on the darting figure who had robbed him of something more precious than his purse.

Then he screamed once, loudly, and fell toward the pavement of the square . . .

TWO

The insistent buzzing of the communicator brought David Holland out of a fitful doze. He rubbed his eyes and sat up in his chair, blinking rapidly as he looked around.

"Uff?" he asked of the empty room, but the only reply came from the buzzing screen on his desk. His shoulders ached, his body further protesting the uncomfortable sleeping position of his nap with a sharp pain in his right calf.

The recognition of his office chased away the last fragments of Holland's nightmare. He rubbed his lower leg as he called the communicator into life, then brushed a scant strand of his thinning gray hair from his forehead.

The flashing red urgent swirl resolved into the face of a technician, staring at something beyond the screen while he waited for acknowledgment.

"What is it?" snapped Holland.

"Sorry to bother you, David." The man seemed imperturbable. "But you wanted to be informed as soon as the test run was finished."

"Oh. Yes." Holland's face reddened at his own irritability. His tiredness was no excuse for forgetting his own orders. The technician diplomatically failed to meet the focus of David's eyes.

"I'm sorry, Nathan—I'll be right down."

Holland stood, a man descending the far side of middle-age, his stocky trunk as gnarled as an old oak. His body completed the final adjustment from the world of fitful dreams, and his surliness evaporated. The tiredness was left, however, and he glanced at the desk clock—2 A.M. He had slept little more than an hour, and that the first after being at his office for the past forty hours without break.

He smelled himself then, and felt the grime on his forehead and his cheeks. He moved into his private 'fresher stall, dashing cold water over his face. He shook his head, forcing his eyes wide open, and stuck his face under the tap. By the time he had to come up for air the dull ache in his temples was subsiding, and he was beginning to feel almost human.

He yawned again, glancing hungrily at the couch a bare meter away from the desk. For a moment he stopped by the desk again, as though looking for something. But the desk was bare of anything but the communicator, and a true cube of his son.

His eyes caught the artificial ones of the boy, Clay, his knuckles for a moment touching the polished veneer of the wood. The picture had been taken for the class yeartape just a few months before graduation, and showed him at his most adolescent. He was smiling and eager, looking impossibly young, the immaturity heightened by the silly gold and silver clan mark on his left cheek.

Holland remembered the last time he had seen Clay, a month ago, just prior to his departure for distant Karyllia. He still seemed very young, but the half year between the picture and graduation had been enough to mature him so that he no longer seemed a mere boy.

For a moment David was sick with his longing for the lad, wishing that he was with him across the stars. Then he sighed and left the office.

He stepped into his private drop shaft, and then out again at the third sublevel. The half dozen technicians working the same extended shift that had kept him from his bed looked up at Holland's entrance but kept at their tasks, too busy to stop.

Nathan came over, a pinch-nosed young man with old-fashioned rimmed spectacles perched halfway down his nose. He carried a computer print-out, handing it to Holland, the technician seeming harried.

"We're still running the rechecks, David, but these are the final results of the first run."

"Is everything satisfactory?" asked Holland, accepting the sheets. Nathan shrugged.

"Most everything."

Holland looked up sharply at the qualification, studying the technician closely. For the first time he noticed that Nathan had been losing weight. The man was almost cadaverously thin, and there was a decidedly unhealthy pallor underlying his skin. Yet he seemed flushed, as though a fever were burning. Was he starving himself?

If he were, it was nonsense. Even though there was little arable land left on the surface of the planet, the space farms could feed the entire population of Earth twice over. They had been started as an experimental program during the Great Famines and the resulting Nuclear War, coming into full development too late to save the 80 per cent of Earth's population that had died during those decades. The nukes took care of perhaps a quarter of that number. Starvation and accompanying disease accounted for the greater amount.

The farms had been there to save the rest, however, and through the centuries had expanded with the once-again increasing population. Now only exotics were grown on the planet's surface.

Holland made a note to have Janice check into Nathan's condition. She watched over the health of the staff along with her other duties. Perhaps she had already noticed the change; she was usually the first to become aware of such matters, bringing them to Holland's attention.

He looked around, saw that she was absent. "Where's Janice?"

"Here, David." His wife came out of the next room, carrying an infant. "Feeding time."

Holland grunted as she adjusted her red-faced burden, bringing it over for his inspection. He peeked dutifully at the wrinkled face as Janice pulled the blanket out of the way briefly, then quickly looked away again. The physical details of caring

for his ultimate charges always seemed to embarrass him, and
Janice smiled with secret amusement as he backed away.

He focused his attention on the sheet in his hand, skimming
the body of the contents as he looked for the anomaly
suggested by Nathan's qualification. Everything seemed to be
following the ideal model laid out in blue beneath the new
traceries—and then he came to the series of cardiograph read-
outs.

"Strong murmur," he said, tapping the sheet and staring at
the technician. "What happened?"

Nathan shrugged. "An imbalance in the input—which you
bloody well know means that I haven't the foggiest, David. It's
the only off-sign in the entire run."

Holland shook his head, angry. "It shouldn't have happened
—not with everything else so close to ideal. Someone was asleep
at the wrong moment." He stared at Nathan as though he were
directly to blame.

"Cool down, David," said Janice. "Your ears are turning red
again."

She handed the child to one of the woman technicians after
passing up the chance to give it into male hands, and came
over to her husband. She pulled the print-out from his fingers
and tossed it toward the nearest bench.

"We're all tired," she said. "Overtired. Once the child is
transferred to the crèche, I vote a thirty-day holiday for the entire staff."

"Impossible." Holland shook his head, going to the small
steno desk in the corner to sit down. He sighed, arching his
back and stretching out his arms, fingers curving upward as he
tried to release some of the tension. "Budget's coming up again
next week—Senator Wiley's forcing another review of the program."

"Are you sure?" asked his wife, concerned.

"The message was waiting when I got upstairs." He
shrugged. "I didn't bother to call you, knew the bad news
would be out soon enough."

"It's only been six months since the last review," said Nathan. "What are they looking for?"

"Political hay," said David. "But holidays are out for everybody. If anyone is presently scheduled to start one, you've just been canceled. We need every able-bodied hand at full work until after the snoops finish their sweep. After, maybe we can cut back for a bit, all of us relax. But even then I'll want to get the next program going right away."

"Is that wise?" Janice glanced toward the child.

"We've no time to waste," he replied.

His wife shook her head. "We've been talking, David, the staff, and we think we should hold off on the next program, perhaps even dismantle the system to its base and build from the bottom up again. There is no way we can know for sure, but it could well be that the present defect is the fault of the network rather than of the input."

"Is that a formal recommendation?"

"It can be put in writing, if you insist."

Holland swiveled to look at Nathan again, but the man managed to avoid his eyes. In profile, the technician's eyes seemed to glisten unusually bright.

"If you tear down the system, can you cover it against a sweep?" he asked.

"We've done it before," said Janice.

"Yes, but we've never been in this tight a situation before," reminded her husband. "This is not going to be a rub the hand over the counter and look at the computer balance sort of check. Their hearts will be in it, and the very best sherlocks the government can supply."

He stifled a yawn and sighed, staring at a shuffle of paperwork on the desk in obvious distaste. His wife studied him for a moment, concerned by the fatigue lines that were marking him an old man.

"You really think we have to fear them this time, don't you, David?"

"Ah, I think too damn much, that's my problem."

He shrugged, slamming his hand against the desk. "Wiley is

a blowhard, but his jumping to the Reformationists shows that we've been seriously underestimating their strength. There will be more defections from the party, count on it—right down the centrist line. I'm sure now that there will be a new majority label controlling the council after the next election."

"But still the same old politicians," his wife countered.

"No," said David. "Not the same old hacks. This time we have something that hasn't been seen since the Bad Years. With the Humanity Firsters on the streets and the Reformationists in the government, the time of the demagogue has come again."

Suddenly the infant began to squall as the woman holding it tried to still the upset. The child continued to cry, however, and Janice took it back from her, bringing the baby over to the desk, sitting on the edge.

Holland stared up at the red face as his wife jiggled the infant in her arms. As always, he was struck by the innate helplessness of the newborn—and felt helpless himself in the face of a crisis that was domestic in nature. He essayed a smile, which did not come out as intended, and even though he knew that the child's eyes could not focus on him, was rewarded by a renewal of outrage.

His wife did smile, turning away, the baby magically subsiding as soon as it was sheltered from the director of the Project. She placed the child in a bassinet and turned it over to the woman again, who wheeled the conveyance from the lab. Holland stared at the woman's back, happy to see her going.

He always tried his best to conceal his true feelings about the children, but with no success so far as Janice was concerned. Still, the importance of the project made him try each new time to overcome his natural aversion.

Politics; it was an old game, but now it actually threatened the future of the race. It was a scientific fact that the level of human intelligence had been diminishing at a rate that was both clearly measurable and increasing. Once the average mind had brought the race out of cave darkness and started man on his path to the stars, but now the individual at median level could not even care for himself without an outside guiding hand. Drones the majority of the race had become, in truth as in derogatory appellation. And there was a limit to how much the custodians could do for their uncaring, undemanding wards.

The projections were clear: another five or six generations of deterioration at the present rate, and there would be no custodians left. There would be only the morons, incapable of operating even the machinery of war as they degenerated back to the animal level. The Bad Years would come again, with or without nuclear poisons blowing over the face of the planet. And this time they would stay.

Holland yawned again, acknowledging his own tiredness and knowing that the others were as fatigued as himself. But until the extended series of tests on the newborn child was completed and analyzed there could be no rest for any of the Project cadre. For them, the line separating success from failure was as thin as the line separating life itself from the reality of death.

The tests passed the judgment of life over the newborn, and by no means could all of the children pass. Usually a breakdown was spotted early, the fetus monstrous from the very beginning. Few of those survived to term.

But sometimes the failure was a small one, a defect that could pass almost unnoticed. If it were a surface matter, a blemish or a limb a few centimeters shorter than its mate, little harm would be done. Sometimes, however, even a minor flaw could produce a fatal defect in the developing personality.

This particular child would make it, though, despite the defective heart valve that caused the murmur. If they were really lucky, corrective surgery would repair that damage so that the child might still qualify as a prime candidate. If not, it would undoubtedly grow up to be a useful, functioning member of society—one of the custodians for the next generations.

The hope was always for prime clearance each time that another life came to term, even though the percentage of such total successes was almost vanishingly small. Still, things could go right sometimes, and the successes were what kept the staff to their dedication, kept them working through failure after failure.

This child was almost-right, and this time David Holland was relieved of the necessity of signing the red-bordered slip that meant cancellation of a failed experiment. Over the years there had been many times when he had been forced to initial such an order. Each time the burden of following guilt seemed unbearable, until it seemed as though he could not bear another stroke laid to his personal torment. One of these times, he knew, he would break . . .

He thought again of his son, dedicated to bringing another race to the stars at the time when man was in danger of losing them for himself. Would Clay's work be more successful than his father's?

David Holland had always known that the probability of success in his program was scant at best, and long ago had opted against escape. Suicide would be an easy way out, but his moral construction was such that he could not leave his responsibilities to another. It was a most terrible burden, for it was almost certain that the survival of human intelligence, of the race as rational, thinking organisms, depended on the work of this one Project. . . .

A Project outlawed for three centuries.

Holland tried to shake off depression. This child would live to successful adulthood, and in a week there would be another birthing. One birth a week was not enough, but it was all they could manage at present—until they proved success.

The black mood refused to lift. The burden of guilt was too great to ease his conscience from the long series of high crimes against his own race. Without David Holland, man might indeed sink into the morass . . .

With him, the race might well die.

THREE

Clay woke to the dying ebb of a headache that seemed to have spread over his entire body. He lay still a moment, afraid to open his eyes, and decided that no, the aching was confined to his bones, his skeletal structure. Then he shifted position, his shoulder striking the wall—and new pain exploded through the soft parts of his body.

Air rushed from his lips as he swallowed a scream, his hands clawing at an unyielding surface. He opened his eyes. He was staring at a ceiling that seemed to be made of rushes, although light was feeble. But as he dragged one foot up toward his mid-body, twisting his trunk again, the first pain diminished, became almost bearable.

He gulped chilled air through open lips, his stomach suddenly growling and rolling. The hunger pang was sharp; he was completely empty, which meant that he had been out for at least twelve hours.

He turned his head to look at the opposite wall. He was lying on a high pallet that was barely long enough for him, covered by a single rough-textured blanket. The room was no more than a slot in the thick wall, two meters wide, three meters deep, three meters tall. Crudely dyed hangings covered the door, and the only illumination came from a smoking oil lamp on a high shelf.

The bed was little more than a padded wooden slab. The only other furnishing in the room was a tall pedestal bearing a washbowl.

Clay sat up, feet dangling over the edge of the pallet but still centimeters from touching the floor. His outer robes had been stripped away, leaving him wearing only the short tunic that was the standard off-worlder's protection against the rough native fabric, preventing constant chafing and crotch itch.

The ambient air temperature was no more than fifteen degrees above the freezing point, and he shivered. But before he could do anything the hangings were swept back and a young woman in the robes of a temple servitor entered. She carried a silver tray that bore a steaming bowl.

"Good day," she said, her voice musical.

"Good day," he returned—and then Clay realized that she spoke in Standard. She was short, and looked like a native. As such, she was an attractive specimen of her race. If she were Terran, however, an agent like himself, then the fortune of beauty had evaded her.

"I'm cold," Clay said. "Where are my clothes?"

"The night winds from the plains are always cold," said the girl, placing the tray at the foot of the pallet. She bent to bring his robe from a shelf beneath the bed.

"Night?" Clay seized on the word, comparing it with his physical state. "How long have I been here?"

"More than a day. I was not on duty when they carried you in, but I understand that it was at evening services. Perhaps thirty hours."

He digested the information, dropping to the floor—and immediately regretted the movement. The stone blocks of the floor seemed coated with hoarfrost. He danced a bit as he slipped into the robe, then found his fleece-lined boots on the same shelf. The girl laughed, gently, as he jumped back onto the pallet to finish dressing.

"Winter is almost upon us," she said. "Fortunately the season is a short one."

"What happened to me?" asked Clay, picking up the bowl containing his breakfast. It appeared to be a plain meal cereal, but when he brought the spoon to his lips he found the taste sweetened, nutlike. It was pleasant, satisfying to his empty stomach, and he ate quickly.

"You were felled by the subsonics generated by the Sanctum during call to evening service," said the girl.

The thief. "My filters were stolen."

"More than that," she said. "Your shield transplants were never activated. They were shut off when the doctor checked you."

Clay touched the large bone behind his right ear, pressing gently. He could feel the outline of the tiny box that had replaced a circular centimeter chip of bone. The box contained a communicator good over a short range, perhaps a dozen kilometers. A similar transplant behind his left ear contained the shield, which was supposed to protect against the sonic generators that were the only ancient scientific device known on Karyllia. At close range, however, so near to the source, the shield needed supplementation; thus the filters.

There was no question now that this girl was a fellow agent. No Karyllian would have been privy to the secrets of the shield transplant, although natives were used wherever possible as servants and servitors, masking the underlying secrets of the temple.

"The shields checked out on Earth," said Clay.

The girl shrugged. "They weren't defective—they just were not switched on."

The shields worked before he left Academy, taking ship to Karyllia. The switches were electronic rather than mechanical—which meant that deactivation could only have taken place during the weeks he spent at the space station in final orientation. It must have been done during one of the medical or equipment checks—but deliberately? or by accident?

It must be the latter, Clay decided. Why would anyone wish him harm?

"I'm in the temple?" he asked, although the answer was obvious. The girl smiled, a motherly creature, although she could scarcely have been more than a year or so older than Clay. He tried to remember anyone like her at Academy, but could not.

"Martin managed to bring you within the temple screen, although he threw out his back in the effort. It is quite fortunate for you that his appearance belies his ability."

She picked up the now empty bowl, placed it back on the tray, and started to leave. Clay jumped to the floor again, protesting.

"Hey, don't just walk off!"

She seemed amused. "You'll have another visitor soon enough."

She backed through the hangings as Clay realized that she hadn't given him her name. He pushed through after her to find that he was in a low-ceilinged corridor. This side was lined with a long row of cubicles just like the one he had just left, but the other wall was blank.

There was no sign of the girl, although it did not seem possible that she could have disappeared so quickly. He held up the hangings on the cubicles nearest his own, but they were all in darkness, apparently empty.

The light level in the corridor was almost as bad as in the little room, illumination coming only from smoking torches in iron brackets, some of which had exhausted their oil soakings. Clay moved along the corridor for perhaps fifty paces, the first pain of awakening now diminished to where it could be ignored. The corridor bent sharply to the right, although not at a ninety-degree angle. When Clay looked down the new length, it seemed to be exactly like the section he had just left.

Not ready to start an exploration of the building on his own, he returned to his cubicle. There he looked the little cell over carefully, but saw nothing more obvious than that noticed earlier. The long shelf beneath the bed now held nothing more than two native blankets and a lidded oval pottery container. He lifted the lid and smelled disinfectant, but it was several minutes before he realized the importance of the chamber pot.

The place seemed to be exactly what its appearance implied. Which did not say that he was not under constant monitoring, but he lacked the instruments with which to make even the simplest sweep of the room. His curiosity not satisfied but his explorations completed for the moment, Clay pulled himself back onto the bed to await the coming of the promised visitor.

Clay was instantly aware, watching from hooded eyes, as a priest entered the cell. Like himself, the man was far taller than the average native, although most of the Earthmen on the planet had been selected, like the girl he had met earlier, to blend in with the local races. But the supply of trained agents was not sufficient to permit a total adherence to the ideal. The newcomer was cowled, unusual here within the temple proper, Clay knew. Then he recognized something familiar about the form, even though the face remained hidden. He stiffened in surprise.

"Peter?"

The cowl was swept back, the man revealed smiling. "I should have known better than to try to fool you, Clay."

"But . . . I thought you were back on Earth."

Peter Stone shrugged; he was a close friend of Clay's parents. All of Clay's memories of childhood included Stone as a part of the family grouping, with the Hollands more often than not.

"I assure you that I'm not here because of my insatiable desire for field duty," said Stone. "However, certain matters appear to be coming to a head, and there are those on Earth who thought the place to counteract them was here on Karyllia."

"That makes no sense," said Clay.

"It does to a politician. Come, let's get out of here, to some place warmer if not more comfortable."

Clay jumped down from the pallet, wincing. "Are all the beds here this hard?"

"Eh. Oh no—not quite. I believe it was the medic's decision to leave you on the slab. You can have a tick tonight, though you'll scarcely find it an improvement."

Clay followed the older man along the corridor and through a maze of twists and turns and dips, although very shortly he could not have said whether they were descending into the depths of the building or rising into the walls. They passed apparent natives dressed in servitors' robes, who bowed their heads in respect as they saw Stone's priestly robes. None of them spoke, however, and Clay could not guess whether they were natives or agents.

Then they descended a long flight of steps, coming out at last into a large common room. It was filled with rough tables, the walls lined with both upholstered and plain benches; a few priests lounged in the area. Stone paused to speak to a man at a small table by the entrance, then led Clay farther, into an office that was little more than another cell, although much larger.

"None of the comforts of home, Clay," said Stone, sitting behind a rough-hewn table. He motioned the youth to a crude wooden chair, and leaned back. "Well. I suppose you think explanations are in order."

Clay shrugged. "Unless you have reason to keep me ignorant."

Stone chuckled, then said, "What do you know of the present political situation back on Earth, Clay?"

Clay blinked, the question taking him by surprise. He shook his head. "Little enough—what we've been taught in sociometrics, and what I've picked up from the entertainment tapes, I suppose."

"Historically," said Stone, "politics has been a game, although one played by a very dirty set of rules. Politicians heed the call to power, although few of them can properly handle it. Some years back the psychometricians ran a test program on the entire council, and found that every member of it was sociologically unsuited to a position of control. Needless to say, that report was never published."

Clay listened intently, comfortable in Stone's presence. As a child he had early turned his eyes to the stars, but his first ambition had been toward the probe teams, searching out new systems and new worlds. He knew that the man across the desk had been instrumental in turning him to his present field, although he could not recall at what age he had decided to become a Guide Agent.

Stone had always been connected with Academy, and there had been two periods of more than a year each when he had

vanished from sight. He had never made explanations for his
absences, but now Clay realized that he had been on field duty
on either Karyllia or Locane. The boy grew used to the inter-
ludes, Stone suddenly absent and then perhaps fifteen months
later suddenly back.

"What do you know of the Reformationists?"

Clay shrugged. "Capital libertarians, some such nonsense.
Aren't they the ones who wish to restore the rights of individuals to hold property?"

"That is one of their stated goals."

"They're very noisy," said Clay, recalling news tapes. "They
seem to like stirring up the drones, always disrupting public
meetings—usually those which are none of their business. I'm
amazed that the leaders of the organization have not been
Declassified."

"There are powerful men among them," said Stone. "The
Reformationists are winning many adherents among the producing classes, and it seems likely that they will be naming the
new government after the next elections. What do you know of
the Humanity Firsters?"

"Crackpots," said Clay, without hesitation. "Opposed to star
flight, the Guided Worlds policy, and, I suppose, rain on
Sunday."

Stone smiled. "Close enough—in fact, a very good description of their public activity. The Firsters would appear to be
classic aginers, the outs as opposed to the elitist ins."

He shifted in his chair, crossing his legs and folding his
hands over his knees. "The Firsters may very well be crackpots
in nature, Clay, but they are also dangerous. More important,
and more dangerous, they are very closely allied to the Reformationist party."

"That lacks logic," said Clay.

"Nevertheless, it is true. There is no obvious public connec-
tion, but it exists. The Firsters are the front for the true aim of
the Reformationists. Even though you think the Reformationists are noisy, the Firsters are the activists—the Reforma-

tionists are the planners. Together they wish to create a new order in the human-dominated worlds of the galaxy."

"Except for the colonies, there are no such worlds," said Clay.

"They count Karyllia and Locane with the colonies," said Stone.

"Mm." Clay thought over Stone's words. "What effect does that have on us, on our role here? The Agency is forbidden by the Compact from being involved with the internal matters of Earth."

"The Agency is restricted, Clay, but we as individuals have not lost our rights as citizens. Ours is a free society to those competent enough to win and hold the franchise, and any citizen is free to engage in political activity. Karyllia is of the utmost importance, I assure you, to the plans of both the Reformationists and the Firsters."

"I still don't understand," said the younger man.

"The Firsters are not just spouting rhetoric, Clay—they mean what they say in their proclamations. They very much believe that there is room in the galaxy for only one race of man —Earthman. It is their intention to destroy every intelligence that threatens competition with Earth's dominance."

Stone seemed suddenly aged. "The Firsters do not want Contact between the races. They will not—cannot—permit us to succeed here, or on Locane. They are not gentle in their opposition—even now they are planning a bloodbath that will scourge the face of both guided planets."

FOUR

David Holland felt a gentle touch on his arm and shifted, pulling away. Sleep still held him lightly as the touch came again, and he refused the summons, eyes still closed tightly. He turned on his side, reaching for his pillow to pull it over his head.

"David!" The touch was more insistent, tugging, and now the smell of Janice's perfume tickled the fine hairs in his nostrils. She called him again.

"Uff! Go 'way! What time is it?" Holland screwed up one eye, but from this position couldn't see a clock.

"Seventeen hundred," replied Janice. "We've slept half the clock away, David."

It had been nearly 0500 when they finally made it to bed this morning; this was the first time in weeks that Holland had managed a complete sleep cycle without interruption. The extra five hours were an unexpected bonus, and now he felt lazy.

"I like it here," he said. "I'm not going to get up until next week."

"Oh yes you are," said Janice. "We have to be at the Letermeisters in an hour for the buffet, and you know how Charles is when people are late."

"Umm." He acknowledged the statement by throwing back the cover, but it was a minute before he sat up. "Another political affair—you know how I hate them."

Janice had begun to dress. "All of Charles's affairs are political, David. Now hurry and shower, and you can have ten minutes on the table. I've already keyed it—a massage will do you good."

Holland felt good as he stood, stretching the last sleep from his body. The sense of well-being was rare, but if a single satisfying sleep could produce it he'd have to try and reorder his routine to permit it more often. The problems of the lab and the Project seemed far away at the moment.

A stiff evening breeze was blowing the curtains into the room. Holland made his way around his side of the bed, his movements automatic as he avoided the articles of furniture intruding into the limited area. He paused by the glass doors to the balcony, leaning to grasp the rail, his eyes sweeping out across the Bay of Fundy. The air was unusually clear as autumn evening approached; he could see the hazy line that was Nova Scotia, fifty-five kilometers away.

Below, there was nothing between this line of buildings and the white sand beach except the ten-meter wall that cut off the noncitizens of New Brunswick from the pleasures of the water. The beach had been painstakingly built to serve the privileged classes of the district only.

As holders of the yellow, David and Janice Holland were of the very highest citizen class and entitled to such special privileges as this exclusive apartment, which contained nearly thirty square meters in its three rooms. When Clay had entered school his father opted to pay the extra tax and keep the boy's room as a study. It was a decision he occasionally regretted, for during the years he had rarely been able to enjoy the private space.

Only the most highly placed members of the government ranked higher than holders of the yellow, and even they had no more personal space than the Hollands.

David went into the 'fresher to dial his shower. A quick cycle of hot, cold, and then gentle warm, and he came out of the needle spray feeling years younger. A sharp aroma came to his nostrils as he stretched out on the table and let the robot fingers begin the massage, he sniffed, hungrily. Then it was gone, and he decided that he must have been wrong. His stomach reminded him that he had not eaten before going to bed, however, and when he came out of the 'fresher he was pleased to see Janice setting two places at the small table at the foot of the bed.

Then the aroma hit him again, and he grinned happily.

"Coffee! Real coffee—have you been trading on the black market?"

"I've been hoarding a half-kilo," she replied, pouring his cup full.

"For how long?" he demanded.

She smiled. "Long enough. I can't think of a better time to use it, David. The stimulant will help us keep our wits tonight, and I think perhaps I should bring it down to the lab. We'll certainly need it this next week, during the sweep."

Holland sat down eagerly, reaching for the cup and taking a satisfying mouthful. It had been years since there had been a decent coffee crop—it was one of the plants that refused to adapt to conditions in space, so that it was now strictly a high luxury item. He recalled hearing that there was only one plantation left now, which probably meant that the crop was reserved for government officials.

"Is this all?" he said, dismayed, as he surveyed the single soya cutlet on his plate and the small glass of citric blend. "I'm hungry, Janice!"

"You'll be nibbling all evening at the buffet," she said, firmly. "You always have food in your fingers at these affairs."

"A defense mechanism," he said, after draining the glass and while cutting the cutlet. "If my mouth is full, I don't have to make idiot conversation."

"You should make more conversation," said his wife. "It won't hurt to have friends at court."

"We have friends," he said. "Charles is my friend."

"Fortunately for the Project, yes. However, he is also Commissioner of Science, and holds a seat at the President's Table. Charles Letermeister is only one man, and it would help to have some of the other commissioners on our side."

It was an old argument, and one that Holland now shrugged

off. He rose, wiping his lips, and started to dress for the evening, the breeze uncomfortably cool on his naked skin as the sun started to set. Janice had changed while he was in the 'fresher; now she cleared the table, made final adjustments to her make-up and coiffure, and was ready as her husband summoned their evening capes from the closet.

He called for an aircar and they took the lifttube to the roof. Another couple was waiting in the pavilion; Holland vaguely recognized them, thought the fellow was a factory manager or something of the sort. If so, he held no higher than green, and that meant that they had less space in their apartment than the Hollands, and a view over the city of St. John rather than the bay.

Holland nodded, and a moment later they were gone in their aircar. Janice shook her head.

"They think we're terrible snobs, David."

"Eh? Why? We've given them no reason to think that."

"No, and no reason to think otherwise. At the buffet try not to consider every stranger automatically an enemy, please. For me, if not for yourself."

He shrugged, agreeing, thinking that he had little time for social amenities, and even less interest. Then the car was there and they climbed in, Holland presenting his ID and the address to the robot controller. A moment later they were moving over the towers of the city toward Government Center.

As soon as she was seated Janice reached to turn on the citizen's channel on the communicator. A bored young woman was reading the district weather forecast; Holland scarcely glanced at the screen. It had been years since he had fallen out of the habit of watching, too busy to have time for leisure activities of even a sedentary nature.

But he felt good now. He looked at his wife, saying, "I think your idea of a general holiday is a good one. It's been years since I've had the chance to do any skiing—what say we apply for passes to the Andes?"

She smiled, patting his hand. "If you like, David."

Holland glanced at the screen again, distracted by the switch to a news reader, a man. He disappeared a moment later, replaced by another woman. They all seemed to possess the same droning monotone. At that, though, it was better than listening to the mindless pap spewing out of the public channel. The drivel for the drones poured twenty-four hours a day out of the main communication satellite, for even as the approaching night brought lights out to a district's barracks, eight hours to the east another district was waking to the same mindless pacifier.

The sun was nearly gone now in the west, the canyons of the city deep in darkness; only the highest towers were still touched by the rapidly vanishing rays. Then the screen suddenly switched to a street location, where a torchlight demonstration was being held. The camera was far back, but the sound of the crowd's yells was a steady background roar to the commentator's voice.

"It's the Humanity Firsters," said Janice. "They're at Government Center, David."

Holland grunted. "From the looks of the crowd, the Firsters' goons must have swept the nearest barracks clean. Turn it off."

"We should hear what they're saying," his wife protested.

"They're screaming what they always scream," said her husband. "Simpletons, the lot of them."

The question became moot as the car passed over the protective screen around the government building complex and settled toward the roof port. For a moment David could see the crowd in the street, and then they were in darkness. As he and Janice stepped out of the car there was only a distant muted sound that might have been the crowd's roar.

Holland shrugged, steeling himself for the ordeal ahead as he took Janice's cape and handed the two outer garments to a robot checker, accepting a claim button in return. Then they went into the drop shafts, coming out some twenty floors below where the main reception hall was located. The lobby was broad and high-ceilinged, the tiled floor sprouting innumerable tall pots of greenery.

There was a human greeting the guests at the entrance to the reception suite, a holder of the lowest classification of citizenship, the blue. There were millions as qualified in the barracks, although few were needed to do the minimum amount of work that required human hands but no particular intelligence. The rewards of the blue were small compared to the benefices of the upper classes, but still a giant leap above the dismal life of the drones.

Most of the workers on Holland's staff were technicians, and entitled to the rose cards, which in status were only just above the blue. But they were the ones who actually kept the machinery of society running, and for those qualified enough, or adept enough at politics, there was the chance to rise through the classes to the green and even the yellow.

Janice had started as a rose, while Holland himself had been an orange, picked out at birth for indicated potential that proved itself quickly when he finally entered school. He was a born administrator, and had served in several capacities while still very young. For the past thirty years, however, he had been in charge of the Project, placed there by his friendship with Charles Letermeister.

Who came forward to greet them now. He bowed low in a courtly manner, taking Janice's hand in his own and touching his other fingers to the back of it.

"Janice, David. So happy you could come."

"As though we had a choice, Charles," said Janice, smiling. Letermeister shrugged.

"Do any of us have a choice, ever? Wiley is already here."

He indicated a direction with a nod, and the Hollands followed the gesture to see the tall, patrician head of Senator Wiley in the middle of an active group. He was looking their way, and nodded, smiling. Then he turned away, his attention caught by one of those about him.

"The senator's staff have been pressing my department," said Letermeister. "The old fox has wind of something, you may be sure."

"About the Project?" Janice asked, quickly.

"I wish I knew." He shrugged again, and then his eye was

caught by newer arrivals. "Excuse me. We'll find time to talk later, David, under the shield."

He was gone then, and Holland found himself in the midst of a drifting mass of humanity. There were several hundred already present, and more arriving every moment; it was beginning to seem as though everyone in the district above the rose had been invited.

He moved toward the buffet tables as Janice had known he would, filling a small plate and at last satisfying his hunger while he nodded greetings at acquaintances and faces that seemed familiar. Janice was more animated, joining in a number of conversations, drifting away for a few moments. Then she came back, her eyes glowing with excitement.

"They're going to dance patterns. Please—come with me!"

He shook his head. "Sorry, my love, but you know that I am completely lacking in co-ordination for such adventures. Here's Charles, he'll dance with you."

Their host came up again, aware that he was the subject of the conversation. When David explained, he nodded and offered his arm to Janice.

"Of course, an honor and a privilege, m' dear."

"Thank you, Charles." She placed her hand on the back of his wrist and he covered it formally with his other fingers. Music was pouring out of the adjoining ballroom as perhaps half of the people began to move in that direction. Already the first template of the pattern was forming, the swirling gowns of the women and the bright peacock colors of the men blending together until an observer from above would have seen only a kaleidoscopic explosion of constantly changing fragments of brilliance.

Holland drifted through the crowd, stopping for a few moments on the fringe of a crowd listening raptly to a minor senator from Sumatra or someplace similar. The bombast was only a drone in David's ears as he studied the faces of the audience, amused by the human capacity for total suspension of credibility. It was too bad that these were not the senator's constituents; his re-election would have been assured in a landslide.

He moved on, was caught for a few minutes by one of Letermeister's assistants, a fellow hoping to make undercommis-
sioner and therefore glad-handing any and all who seemed close
to his superior. For some inexplicable reason he wanted to tell
David about his family, and when Holland finally escaped he
rushed to the buffet to refill his plate.

Two women and a man drifted near, the most voluble ex-
pounding on the near-religious ecstasy of her recent conversion
to the Reformationist movement. The others listened with interest, and attracted the attention of a similar group, which
blended with the first. At last the excitable woman looked toward David, stabbing a finger.

"You, sir—aren't you Dr. David Holland?"

He nodded. "You have the advantage of me, madam."

She ignored the parry. "You're in charge of the program
which supposedly is studying birth defects as caused by the natural mother carrying the fetus to full term."

"Simplified, yes, that is one of the causes presently under investigation."

He looked about, saw Janice staggering slightly as she came
out of the ballroom. The man with her was a youngster, and he
helped her find a chair, the two of them laughing at some private amusement. He turned to snag drinks from a passing
waiter, the robot cart obediently slowing until its dim-witted
sensors decided that it was no longer wanted.

"Isn't that the truth, Doctor."

"Mmm? I beg your pardon, madam?" He blinked, looking
back at the insistent woman.

"I said, isn't the truth of the matter completely different,
that in reality your program is devoted to investigations that
have been forbidden, Doctor, by world compact for nearly
three centuries! Isn't it the truth, Dr. Holland, that far from
being concerned with the problems of childbirth, you are creat-
ing androids?"

The forbidden word stabbed through the small audience,
moving swiftly beyond to catch other ears. People were turning

now, staring in open curiosity as those within earshot began to move closer.

"Well, Doctor?" she persisted. "Can't you answer—or is it that you don't dare answer?"

Stunned by the woman's words, Holland fumbled for an answer, stumbling over his own tongue.

"That statement . . . is utterly preposterous, madam," he managed finally. "Are you insinuating that the Commission of Science would be engaged in illegal research—more, that such research could continue, supported by public funds, for a period of thirty years?"

He glanced around, frantic, looking for help, someone to rescue him. He didn't like dealing with strangers in the best of circumstances, and now he wished that Janice was here. She knew how to blunt the obvious wrath behind such a blatant attack.

"You're avoiding my question, Doctor."

"No, madam." He shook his head. "Not avoiding—simply unable to countenance that it would even be asked. The answer is no, unequivocally and absolutely. My Project is not engaged in android research." **1970460**

"Dr. Holland, I believe you are lying."

The challenge was cold, causing another ripple of excitement. David stared at her, perplexed; what was the witch trying to do, provoke a duel?

"You will note, Doctor," she added at that point, "that I have simply stated an opinion. I have not slandered you, sir."

At that she turned, moving off. Seconds later more than a dozen of the fascinated audience hurried to join her again, their voices buzzing. The few remaining who had heard her stared at David a moment, then moved off themselves.

Feeling a touch of panic, Holland started toward his wife. Before he was more than halfway there Charles Letermeister appeared again, stopping to talk to Janice. They looked up as David arrived.

"Well, here he is now," said Janice. "With an empty plate, as usual. How many times have you refilled it this evening, David?"

He ignored her jibe, setting the plate on the nearest empty chair. "Charles, we must talk now—and under the shield. Now!"

"Of course, David. We can go up to the President's Table. Not even Senator Wiley can disturb us there."

Janice saw the expression on her husband's face and immediately stood. There was no question of her not accompanying them—she was as much the heart of the Project as her husband was its brain center. She caught his arm and started to steer him through the press, the commissioner following a pace behind.

David saw the woman again, making her way through a thick group around Senator Wiley. He raised his hand, and the crowd parted; they conversed, the senator nodding.

He looked in their direction, saw the Hollands with the commissioner, and smiled. He came toward them, intercepting them before they could reach the door.

"Ah, the Doctors Holland! A pleasure, dear madam, dear sir. I'm so glad to see you here tonight—but then, you would never miss an affair hosted by dear Charles, would you?"

"Good evening, Senator," said Janice, taking the lead. "You're looking well."

"Thank you, madam," he said, smiling deeply. Wiley's hair was completely white, his face seamed gently with the lines of age. On his features, the effect was one of an endowed wisdom. "Tell me," he continued, "are you ready to receive my auditors?"

"We are always ready for public inspection," said David. "Our records are open."

"Excellent, Doctor, excellent. Let's see . . ." He glanced at his watch. "Twenty-two thirty, yes. The team should be arriving at your quarters just about now. I do hope your night-duty technician is awake to admit them."

Holland stared, unblinking. "Now?"

"Yes, Doctor, quite probably at this very minute. I know that you were expecting the sweep next week, but I believe that it's best to come when not expected. Not that you have anything to hide, of course . . ."

He chuckled, deprecating his own words. "Well, I suppose you'll want to return to your office now. I think I may just come along myself—may I offer you a lift in my car?"

Again stunned, Holland felt Janice's fingers digging deep into the flesh of his arm. He covered her hand as he shook his head.

"No, Senator. Thank you, but we wouldn't dream of imposing."

"Ah, but that is a fatal weakness, Doctor." The senator wagged a long, bony finger. "I always impose. Good night."

Holland closed his eyes in pain as Wiley moved away. Then Charles touched his arm.

"David, you have nothing to worry about—they can't find anything they shouldn't. Come—let's go under the shield."

He shook his head again. "It's too late, Charles. They already know."

FIVE

On the third day after his arrival at the temple the medic pronounced Clay fit to return to full duty. There was still a little tenderness in his joints, but the constant aching had left his bones and his strength had returned to nearly normal.

"You'll live, this time."

The medic returned his instruments to a much-scarred double-bound leather trunk in the corner of the chilly room; the modern equipment seemed incongruously alien in the primitive setting. The only heat in the temple came from great open fireplaces, which were few in number, or from small brass braziers filled with peat. The first could warm the front side while icicles formed on the back, while the second might have been effective for warming beds if there were some acceptable-to-Karyllia way of preventing the fire from consuming the furniture.

Clay shivered as he adjusted his robes, glad to have even the native coverings. The weather had changed during the past forty-eight hours, a freezing wind now sweeping from the north, losing none of its fury as it crossed the open plains. Clay had thought winter was threatening, and then was informed that such aberrations were typical of the region. The wind could turn again at any moment, and there would be summer heat.

The space station gathered weather information from a series of satellites, but even after fifty years the knowledge of the planet's idiosyncrasies was insufficient to make prediction more than a series of wild guesses.

"Thank you," said Clay, standing. "I'll try not to let it happen a second time."

The medic grunted. "Your shield is working now. You shouldn't have any more problems with the Snakes—at least, not with their sonics."

He snapped a huge padlock shut through the trunk's iron hasp. The true locks, of course, were concealed within the construction, and any attempt to force the trunk by someone with no more than a Karyllian knowledge of locking systems would meet with instant disaster. Should more sophisticated knowledge be applied, the trunk could protect itself to a point, and then would self-destruct . . . taking with it the assaulters.

All of the Terran equipment was similarly protected, concealed within articles of native manufacture. There was surprisingly little in the way of technological support for the mission, however; the agents made do wherever possible with Karyllian equipment. Thus the furnishings of the temple, and of the other Terran outposts on the planet, were strictly as the natives could best produce.

Even the necessary communication equipment, to maintain contact with the space station and with the agents on detached duty, took up far less space than the medical locker. Those items of self-defense an agent might be permitted to use in the final extremity were carefully concealed within prosaic articles of clothing. At the moment Clay was not particularly armed, but his boots carried a supply of grenades—gas in the left, explosive in the right. Other nasties were concealed within his belt and its buckle.

In the field, an agent was a walking arsenal—but woe unto the man who used his weaponry in a manner not later approved by his superiors.

Most of the Terrans on the planet were in the field, of course; there were outposts of the temple in the larger cities, while a certain number of missionaries were traveling the highways in a constant movement that crisscrossed the continent. The number was limited, of course, and over-all a single remote village might not see a priest more often than at harvest time.

Traveling missionary was the role that Clay would shortly be playing, serving as Peter Stone's private double agent.

"I don't know who I can trust," Stone had said. "I only know that our ranks are riddled with the Reformationists. They have been careful in their recruiting, swearing all off-Earth adherents to total secrecy. Yet they do have to recruit, and so there is some overt activity."

"How many are against you?" asked Clay.

Stone shrugged. "I can't even guess. The rot may completely undermine our structure here, it may be contained to a relative few. I have to pretend that I have no knowledge of their activities—I don't dare force them into the open. Not yet. I fear they'll break out sooner than we want in any event."

"Are you certain of any of their members?"

"I suspect everyone, Clay." Stone forced a wry smile. "Even you. But I'm staking my life on you. If you are against me, the game is lost now."

For a moment Clay said nothing. The man sitting across the table was as close to him as his own parents, the ties as strong as family blood. The silence quickly grew heavy, broken at last by the older man.

"Of course, I suspect some more than others—Martin, for one."

"He saved my life," said Clay.

"He doesn't know who you are, Clay." He shrugged. "I know Martin is trying to earn my confidence, he's been working his way to me from the day I arrived. Of course, the man may only be a sycophant by nature, but I wish I could probe him—probe them all."

"There must be probe equipment on the station."

"And a strong possibility that the operator is a Reformationist, or at least a sympathizer."

"If things are so dangerous, should we be talking now? Is this room secure? They must know that you came to greet me as soon as I came to."

"This room is under my personal shield—I swept it myself just before I went to get you. Oh, there are spy bugs enough, but they don't have a generator strong enough to break my barrier. They'd need the power of a navy cruiser, at the least."

He stretched, easing the tension in his back. "As to my greeting you, I've made it my practice to meet every new man as soon as he comes to the temple. I also bring them here for an extensive personal interview; most of them think it's a terrible bore, telling the old man about their families back home and their ambitions. They think I'm dotty, but it serves as an excellent cover."

He rubbed his neck. "I'm tired, Clay—I'm too old for field duty. I need a soft bed at night, somebody warm to hold on to. I hate the cold, the intrigue—when this affair is over I think I'll retire. Assuming the option is left to me."

Clay had been carefully considering the various statements made by the other, all of which had been shocking in one degree or another. It was a minute before the new words registered, and then he looked up, his surprise showing.

"Retire? You?"

How old was Peter Stone? He didn't appear to be out of his seventies, but on the other hand, Clay could never remember him as being any younger. The facial lines had always been there, but the weariness was marked now in the way the eyes seemed to sag in their sockets, the constant droop to the corner of his mouth.

"The Reformationists know that I am their enemy," said Stone, ignoring Clay's shocked question. "I'm a clear target, and thus must walk carefully. I, on the other hand, can't even see them, don't know their location, their military abilities, even the number of their forces. I jump at shadows, swing at the darkness. I work at night without benefit of moon or infrared scanners. Yet I must fight them, must stop them. I need your help."

Clay shrugged. "What can I do?"

"I'm sending you out on a mission, with Martin. Talk to the man, Clay, get to know him. Be sympathetic with the Reformationist cause, be disdainful of the Guided Worlds policy. Be fruit ripened on the vine, ready to be plucked. If we are really lucky, he may try to proselytize you to the cause."

Clay remembered Martin's conversation as they hurried through the streets of Ahd-Abbor, and now he repeated it for Stone's benefit. The agent nodded.

"Still not proof, but helpful. I want to know what Martin does away from the temple—if he tries to contact other agents, what he says to them. Even the way he treats the natives. A push is coming, Clay, I feel it. I want to know in advance when it is ready."

"A bloodbath," said Clay. "Do you expect an invasion from Earth?"

"It's possible, but I doubt it. The logistics would be terribly expensive, even if the Reformationists do manage to take over the government. It would be far easier to subvert a single ship, or even a few men on it, and seed the planet with biologicals. It would be completely safe, and guarantee at least a 90 per cent wipe of the native population. In the cities, with other natural diseases released, the toll would be complete."

Clay shuddered. "It sounds so callous. I can't really believe that men would do that to anyone."

"It's only one possibility," said Stone. "They may have decided to exploit the local populations through slave labor programs. I don't know, Clay; that is the problem!"

Stone rose again, Clay following suit as the older man held out both hands. The youth clasped wrists with him, holding tight for a moment.

"You're my only weapon, Clay," said Peter Stone. "I'm going to use you to stir the hornet's nest into activity. I hope that you don't get stung too badly in the process."

"What if I am invited to join them?" asked Clay. "What do I do?"

"Accept, of course." Stone smiled. "With alacrity."

The mission was set. Clay and Martin would leave the next day at first light while the Terrans in the temple welcomed the rising sun. The dawn ceremony was the most important in the new religion, and with luck, there would be an increase of a score or so natives among the few hundred Karyllian converts to the off-world pantheon.

Clay stood in a side passage looking out at the open space of the main temple now, wondering how many of the natives were there because of religious fervor and how many because of the generous soup kitchen operated by the agents. It made little difference whether they were interested in their stomachs or their souls, as long as their renunciation of the Sanctum was genuine. A large percentage, however, made both the dawn service with the Eternal Light and the twilight service with the Sanctum.

There were half a dozen agent-priests holding vigil, seated together on a long, padded bench before the main altar. The Eternal Light did not demand a generous measure of discomfort and genuine suffering with its worship. In turns, one priest at a time got up and chanted at a lectern.

On another, lower bench at the side of the altar were three servitors, the assistants whose role Clay would assume when he accompanied Martin. There was a small constant movement across the floor of the temple, which was void of any furniture other than the altar benches. The high-arched ceiling caught the chanting voice of the priest and sent it echoing into every corner. The natives crossing the floor were intent on the kitchen at the far side; some of them glanced toward the chanter, but few stopped to listen or went closer to the altar.

Clay moved on, to the entrance, walking out to stand at the top of the steps. His attention was riveted as always on the native Sanctum directly opposite; he had come here a dozen times each day and during the evening to stare at the ancient and terrifying construction of the Snakes.

It bulked little higher than the surrounding houses, but sheer massiveness gave it added stature. Like the Terran competition, the Sanctum was built of solid blocks of basalt. But the front of the building was sheathed with obsidian plates, each a man's arm length in diameter. The plates had been polished and burnished by generations of willing hands until now the stone shone as though alive.

The central third of the temple was the portal, extending out over the square. The stones were fitted so close together that they seemed to be a single giant block which had been carved into the glowering, malignant head of a thrusting snake. The jaws gaped wide so that the worshipers passed between them, the fangs raised to strike, dripping slow drops of venom as servitors fed them from within. The great drops were colored a poisonous yellow, and when the breeze blew across the square it carried the odor of ancient death.

The effect of living malevolence was heightened by burning cauldrons set into the eye sockets; at night they glowed with a deep red hatred. As Clay watched, he was unable to control a tremor in his gut.

"Some researchers think it's a Lost Race artifact."

Clay looked up in surprise; Martin had come out behind him. "Do you believe in the Lost Race?"

"I believe in nothing," said the other. "Even what I can see —it may all be nothing but a holograph. That's why you never see me touching, Holland. I'm afraid I might fall through."

"The temple is . . . astounding," said Clay. "Frightening. There really are no words to describe it."

"It does appear to be the oldest structure on the planet," said Martin. "Except for the citadel, of course. Now those searching for the Lost Race should start there, for my money. According to the Snakes, the Sanctum was created in one instant by the Lord of Outer Darkness."

Staring at it even in the light of midafternoon, Clay could well believe the tales of its construction true.

That evening Stone called Clay and Martin together to his office for a final briefing, a perfunctory reminder of instructions and expectations. He clasped wrists with Clay no longer than with the other—but only the youth felt the strength of his grip.

Clay spent a restless night mulling the morrow, not falling asleep until just a few hours before he was awakened by the same girl he had seen at his first awakening. Several times since he had tried to strike up a conversation with her, to no avail. Her smile was always ready, but she knew every twist and turn in the maze the Terrans had constructed in their temple to confuse and mystify the Karyllians. Clay tried to pursue her, but she always managed to elude him before he had turned half a dozen corners.

She was gone now as quickly as she had come, this time her hands empty; Clay managed to wash in cold water, making his way to the common room to join Martin for breakfast.

As the first rays of the sun touched the front of the temple Clay and the older agent made their way to the stables at the rear of the building. Their mounts were ready for them, native hakyar, cousins to the dak. To Clay, they resembled a crossing of the worst features of the Terran camel and horse, with all of the disgusting habits of the former and none of the attractiveness of the latter.

The beasts were already saddled, high-backed things that crested a fatty hump, while the agents' packs were tied down between their legs. The hakyar kneeled to permit mounting, swaying alarmingly as they rose to all fours again, Clay nearly losing his balance despite the safety strap about his middle.

Martin hid a smile, kicking his mount into movement. The hakyar began to shamble out of the stable at a pace surprisingly fast as Clay followed suit; they were neither running nor trotting, but they were certainly moving faster than a man could walk.

At first it seemed that every step of the beast would dislodge Clay as they moved through the awakening city streets. Then his natural balance found the proper way to lean against the swaying motions, and he settled back against the saddle, thankful that the back was as high as a chair's, even supporting his head. Before they were out of the city he was even dozing in his seat, although from time to time he had to shift the double-pointed native sword that was their most obvious armament into a position where the guard would stop digging into his ribs.

The hakyar rolled through the dusty plains, the early morning chill disappearing as the sun rose higher in the sky. The weather was obviously due for one of its unpredictable changes, and Clay knew that before noon he'd regret the extra tunic he was wearing beneath his robes. It had seemed a good idea at the time, but already the cloth was too heavy for comfort.

An hour away from the city and Ahd-Abbor had dwindled behind them to a low hulking mass that barely peaked above the horizon. An hour after that and it was gone completely. They were still in the capital district, however, the road relatively broad and filled with a great deal of traffic that moved toward the city. Twice they passed dak caravans, the dull creatures slowing the hakyar in the manner of stupid herd animals on every planet. At first there was a constant stream of farm wagons, piled high with produce or skins and usually pulled by a hakyar. More than once, however, the farmer and his wife and even their oldest children were between the traces, laboring to move the product of their land to what they hoped would be a profitable market. The natives never looked up as they tugged at the heavy wooden two-wheeled carts.

By the time the sun was at its zenith even the traffic was sparse, and now the road was much narrower, barely a single track that began to rise with the land. There was no longer room for the two men to ride abreast, Martin moving into the lead.

"How much farther to the first village?" called Clay, conscious of a growing hunger that was accompanied by a growing queasiness. He had seen Martin dig a chunk of bread from his saddlebag, and now he followed suit, washing it down with cool water from his canteen. The filling food settled his stomach's protest.

"It's another three or four hours," said Martin, not bothering to turn. "There'll be a celebration for us tonight, Holland."

"Why?"

"The rurals actually like us, although they pay their tribute to the Snake tax collector when he comes through. But this place is ours, heart and soul—they even cleaned out their Sanctum and turned it into a Temple of the Eternal Light."

"What sort of celebration?" asked Clay, a moment later.

"Traditional, as on every intelligent planet—plenty of wine, women, and song, all of the native sort, of course. Too much, really, particularly of the women."

"The Snakes let the villagers alone to join the temple?" said Clay. "I thought they didn't like our competition."

"There is a witch-doctor type, who represents the powers that be. But even he is willing to share in the goodies we bring. Some of these people really don't take their religion too strong."

The countryside was actually becoming hilly, at least as compared to the plains, although they were moving parallel to the northern mountains. The hakyar crested a rise together, pausing there before plunging down the much steeper grade on the other side.

They had passed the last of the farms in the capital district nearly an hour back. There had been isolated habitations since, but they were self-contained, cut off from distant communication. There was scattered woodland now, and the few houses they did see were usually protected by thick trees. As they passed, Clay had the uncomfortable feeling that they were being watched, although there were no natives in sight and no signs of life in the huts.

Until now the road had been hard-packed, but this soil was looser, of a more sandy composition. The hakyar's footpads pluffed where they had plopped, although there was no discernible difference in the ride.

The road was bending gradually, toward the south; they crested another steep hill and saw before them a shallow valley that was filled with a ragged series of wooded copses, the twisted needle-bearing trees conifers for the most part. Clay yawned, shifting his sword again. He glanced down at the double points, the one really a hook to grab an opponent and pull him off balance. The other point was more of a cutting edge, excellent design for decapitation, according to the Master of

Arms back at Academy—providing the victim's head was already on the block.

Clay was dozing when Martin suddenly halted his beast, the second animal stopping as well by necessity. He sat up, looking around—and then saw the other man staring at the scene of a small but furious battle at the edge of the next woods. Four or five hakyar were circling a single rider, who was putting up a valiant but losing fight.

"Bandits!" said Martin, excited. "Are you game to play hero, Holland?"

Before Clay could answer, the agent was kicking his beast into movement again, forcing the hakyar into a run. Clay's mount followed the lead of the other, both shifting into high gear that had Clay clutching wildly for the reins, his feet kicking higher than his head.

Martin plunged into the melee, his sword circling his head in great swoops. Clay was almost upon the trouble before he regained his balance and managed to draw his own weapon. The bandits turned from playing with their victim, shocked by the intrusion, as the agents' swords tasted first blood.

Clay was astonished when the man nearest him fell in a heap to be trampled by his own plunging mount. He stared dumbfounded at the red stain coloring the first thirty centimeters of the slashing edge—then raised the sword to parry a tremendous sweep from another of the bandits. Instinct took control of his muscles as he forgot everything he had learned in weapons training about the fine point of the Karyllian two-pointed sword—indeed, about swordplay at all.

He chopped at his attacker, then yanked the sword back with both hands, the hook catching the cloth of the other's robe and pulling him along. The man tried to stab at Clay, but Martin's slashing edge came down across his neck and he tumbled into the dust, severed arteries spouting blood although his head was still barely connected to his shoulders. Before Clay could let his eyes drop to follow the man another bandit was there; he was forced to parry again, then drove the slashing point down into the other's midriff, spilling his guts.

Suddenly the final two bandits were fleeing, leaving their fellows dead. The riderless hakyar had moved away from the battle as soon as their saddles lightened, and were now cropping the grass at the side of the road. There were three bodies in the dust, all trampled now, although it made no difference to the souls that had once inhabited them.

Clay wiped his mouth with the back of his hand, and then saw the lone Karyllian who had been trying to stave off the attackers lying beside the road. He untied his safety belt, following Martin's example, and climbed down, wondering with one corner of his mind how the natives had managed to keep their seats without belts.

Martin reached the victim first, kneeling to press two fingers against the native's neck. "He's alive," he said, loosening the robes to check for sign of sword damage. "Correction—*she's* all right."

"A woman?"

"None other. It's obvious why she's wearing the robes of a man—a woman riding alone wouldn't have made an hour out of the city. Assuming she came from there—she is wearing market cloth, not homespun."

Martin stretched the woman out into a more comfortable position as Clay came closer, then stood as the youth stared down at the face. Although it had been dark when he last saw its owner, he recognized it immediately.

It was the little thief who had tried to steal his purse.

SIX

"We can't talk here!"

The Commissioner of Science grabbed the Hollands by their elbows and moved them rapidly through the crowded reception suite. Letermeister ignored the glances of idle curiosity thrown their way, but David Holland was uncomfortably aware of the growing level of interest as they passed from the great room. They crossed the lobby to the drop shafts, but Letermeister steered them into a closed elevator instead.

"Security," he said. "The shafts don't open onto the presidential levels, where the Table is located."

Letermeister seemed to relax a bit as the doors closed and the cage began to rise, although Holland felt uncomfortable in the completely enclosed space as he felt the surge of acceleration in his legs. He glanced at Janice, but she seemed unperturbed by the method of transport, and so he kept his silence.

The elevator slowed, gravity reacting a second late to overcome the energy of the rise as their organs shifted in strange fashion in their body cavities. The door opened, and they stepped out before the eyes of a naval guard, who stiffened to attention as he recognized the person of the commissioner.

There was no one else in the corridor, and all of the high doors leading off it were closed. The walls were hung with a long row of naturalistic portraits.

"The President's suite isn't on this level, is it?" asked Janice, interested despite the seriousness of their present situation.

"No, no," said Letermeister. "Just the Table. Here."

He stopped before a pair of doors that seemed no different than the others in the ranks and pressed his palm to the recognition plate. The door swung open, and he stood aside, letting the Hollands enter a plush conference room before him. High-backed chairs surrounded a long wooden table in the exact center of the room, while heavy draperies covered almost all of the four walls. There were no windows to the world outside, their footsteps hushed as they crossed the carpeting.

"A silence generator," said Letermeister, his voice sounding muted now that he was inside. He closed the doors and sealed them, then turned back to face them.

"Now we're under the shield, David—the strongest units on the planet cover this level and the President's own suite. Now, what did Wiley say to make you think he knows about the android program?"

"It wasn't Wiley himself, Charles."

He told them about the confrontation with the Reformationist woman, Janice and Letermeister listening intently as he described her and those who had clustered about her. The commissioner nodded.

"Oh, it was Wiley, David," he said when Holland finished. "It's his mark, none other. The question now is how much do they really know. The Project is covered, isn't it? What can the sweep uncover?"

Holland shrugged, sitting tiredly in a chair that molded itself to his form. His back was aching, but as he leaned back the robot sensors in the chair diagnosed the tension and began a gentle massaging action that was wonderfully relaxing. He sighed with momentary contentment.

"On the surface, nothing, Charles. It depends on how far they are willing to dig. We're vulnerable in certain areas—you know what the budget restrictions have meant."

"They'll dig deep," said the other. "If they have the scent of android, they'll go as far as necessary. This will be the greatest publicity coup they could have asked—no, there'll be no lack of willingness to pursue the inquiry. But can they *prove* their charges?"

"If they know exactly what to look for, certainly."

Holland looked at this wife, who still stood close to the commissioner. Letermeister unconsciously put out his arm, drawing her close, as Janice chewed on her lower lip—a sure sign that she was close to exploding. She felt the weight of the arm and looked up into Letermeister's eyes, then down at her husband, as though to give him a reassurance that she did not herself feel. She moved to David's side, sat down in the chair next to his.

"Tell me the worst," said Letermeister, hardly aware that she had moved. "In the past, most of your briefings have passed over my head, David—I'm sure you were aware of the fact." He smiled. "I make no pretenses as to my abilities. Like yourself, I am an administrator. Tell me exactly what I should expect in the way of accusations. Exactly what can they prove?"

"The blood tests are our most vulnerable point," said Janice, taking over now that they had moved to the technology of the program. "If they compare the supposed donors with the actual children, the game is up."

"Weren't they compatible?" Letermeister asked, incredulous. "That seems the very simplest precaution, one even I would have taken into consideration."

"Of course," said Janice. "And the parents were compatible, always. However, the cost of developing blood types to match each of the parent-pairs was beyond our ability, Charles. It greatly simplified our work to have all of the children share the same blood grouping."

"Didn't you even try to match the donors to the general type?"

"Not at the beginning," said Holland, bitterly.

"We didn't think of it then," Janice explained. "Remember, Charles, thirty years ago there was no strong exogenetic drive, no Reformationists, no Humanity Firsters. We all knew that we were engaged in illegal research, but the risks simply did not seem that great."

"You're right," said the commissioner. "I'm sorry, Janice. Sometimes it seems as though there never was a time before these last few years, never was a period of peace. Continue."

"For the past twelve years the matching has been compatible

in every possible way, but the first graduates of the program have no better than a statistical chance of matching blood type with the supposed parents."

"Twelve years," mused Letermeister. "If they audit no farther back, we may still be all right." He had forgotten his own pessimism of a moment ago as he clutched at hope.

"They won't stop there," said Holland. "I tell you, they *know!* Wiley is not going to be satisfied with any audit, Charles. He's going to demand a complete examination of the history of the entire Project."

"Are you saying that we can do nothing?"

Holland slowly shook his head, looking at Janice. "I don't see what, Charles."

The commissioner sighed, and there was a moment of shared silence as each was momentarily lost in thought. Then Letermeister shifted position.

"Well, the carrousel is moving, and it seems as though we're along for the ride. I suppose that we had best try to hold to our seats for as long as possible. However, I have the feeling that we're about to be thrown off."

"It's a little late to be concerned for our own skins, isn't it?" asked Janice. She looked again at her husband. "We knew there would be tremendous risks before we started, Charles. We all knew what would happen if word got out before the program succeeded. I'm worried now about the children, what will happen to them."

"Yes, the rewards of the enterprise." Letermeister nodded. "The future promise of the human race. Tell me, Janice—now that they're writing us into the black pages of history's ledger, do you still think the rewards worth the price we've paid?"

"Always," she said, softly, then repeated the word. "Always."

"You know Wiley," said David. "What does he really want, apart from power? What do you think his gang of hoodlums will demand from us?"

"Who can say?" The commissioner shrugged. "Perhaps they'll be lenient, now that you've secured the election for

them. Banishment, perhaps—perhaps no more than forced retirement."

Janice said the word they had all been dreading. "Declassification?"

"Not without a trial!" said David.

"They have cause, David, if they wish to bring charges. It
depends on how much Wiley feels he needs to milk the affair.
It is a possibility, yes."

"You're protected, Charles," said Janice. "There is nothing
to tie you to the actual program."

"There is always guilt by association," said the old man,
showing his age. "It may be sufficient. Officially, of course, I
shall be shocked at Wiley's announcement of your traitorous
activities. I will do everything I can to support you here at the
Table, although it will be little enough, I fear."

He passed his hand across his forehead, then looked up,
blinking as though in pain. Janice noticed the tiny shudder
that passed over Letermeister's spine, looked at her husband to
see if David had seen it as well. He gave no sign that he had.

"All we can do now is wait and hope," said Letermeister.

"And pray," Janice added, softly.

The old man blinked. "Yes. And pray, if that is your convic-
tion. Perhaps an understanding intelligence is listening and can
intervene."

He turned to the door, breaking the seal as David and Janice
stood, standing aside to let them precede him into the corridor.
He followed them to the elevator.

The guard was still standing at rigid attention, the commissioner having failed to release him from his stance. Janice saw
the poor fellow's discomfort and tugged at Letermeister's
sleeve.

"Mm?" He followed her glance. "Oh yes. Relax, young man.
Stand easy, whatever it is you do."

The guard relaxed, his grateful expression following Janice as
the door closed, cutting off her view. They rose to the roof,
where David reclaimed their wraps from the robot while Letermeister summoned an aircar. When Holland turned around he

saw that it was the commissioner's official vehicle, human-chauffeured.

The old man handed Janice into the car, then turned to clasp wrists with David.

"Good luck, both of you."

"Thank you, Charles," said David. "We'll need it, in great measure."

The car lifted, carrying them out across the city's darkness. The street before government center was empty now, the demonstration long since ended. They passed in silence over the night, neither the man nor the woman wishing to express themselves in the company of the blue driver. Minutes later the car dropped again, into the secluded park district which housed the Project's building.

The grassy lawn before the steps of the building seemed crowded with parked aircars as the chauffeur got out to hand Janice and then David down to the ground. The man never spoke, and as Janice passed and looked into his eyes, his gaze was fixed on a point well beyond.

Wiley's senatorial limousine was one of the aircars, also attended by a blue. Two vehicles were marked with the insignia of the citizen's channel, but there were at least three or four other cars as well. The ground lights were not on, so Holland could not be sure of the actual number. But it seemed as though an invasion in force had been mounted against the Project.

They hurried up the steps, Nathan moving out of the shadows at the side of the door to greet them. The technician's hair was tousled, as though he had been roused from sleep, and Janice remembered that he had the night watch this week. At all times one of the staff slept in the lab, in case of malfunction in any of the complex equipment supporting the thirty-six developing lives. Thirty-five now, since the one unit had discharged its placenta yesterday, and as yet a new one had not been started.

They stopped on the steps to talk to Nathan, the technician rubbing tension from his neck.

"The first thing they asked for was the donor lists."

"Current?" asked Janice.

Nathan shook his head. "Complete."

Only a sinking feeling in his gut made David Holland realize that for a moment his hopes had been raised. Now he sighed, resigned.

"Then they know exactly what they're looking for."

"How did they find out?" the younger man demanded. "What source told them? It must have been someone connected to the Project!"

Holland shrugged. "It could be anyone; it doesn't matter now. The Reformationists are drawing their sympathizers from every level of citizen, Nathan, and this can only help them grow stronger. For us, the damage has been done. All we can do is try to pick up the pieces."

They moved on into the building's tiny lobby, which was filled to overcrowding now with half a dozen of Wiley's hangers-on. The senator himself was standing in the center of the group, listening attentively to an apparently complicated question being asked by a reporter. Holland saw at least three cameramen, one poking his instrument into every corner of the lobby and opening any door that was not locked, as though the secrets of the Project were waiting to be discovered in a closet.

"Ah, Dr. Holland! This young lady has been waiting for you."

Wiley had spotted them, of course, and now he was waving a hand in their direction. One of the cameramen immediately swung around to focus on the new point of interest, responding to the tiny voice that spoke inside his left ear. He zoomed in on David and Janice as the reporter reluctantly turned from the senator. A look of distaste came over her face as she saw the director of the Project.

"You will forgive the upset," said the senator, moving closer. "I'm afraid the sherlocks have taken over your office, Doctor, but they'll be moving out in the morning, as soon as their own librarian units can be brought in. I hope this doesn't inconvenience you unduly, but perhaps you can find space for them."

"Of course," said David, stiffly, determined to play the charade according to the other's rules. "I have nothing to hide, Senator."

"Nothing?"

The reporter captured his words, throwing them back at him, moving in now to challenge. "Do you deny, Dr. Holland, the rumors that your Project has been engaged in forbidden research—that indeed, it has been so engaged from the moment that it was established?"

Holland chose his words carefully. "I find it incredible that such accusations have been made."

"Then you claim that you are not engaged in android research?" pressed the girl. "You say that you have not been constructing androids in your laboratories?"

Each time she said the word the distaste returned to her expression. Holland forced a smile, turning slightly to look directly into the camera.

"This is scarcely a factory. We are not *making* anything. At present we are engaged in carrying out several different studies into the entire problem of birth defects. I'm sure that everyone listening knows the seriousness of this matter. Ever since the Bad Years the incidence of unviable mutation has been steadily increasing in natural childbirth. Our work here is of the utmost importance if we are ever to save millions of women from this tragic failure."

"You are not making androids, then."

"We are researching human life."

"*Human* life—not artificial?"

"I'm sure I don't know what you mean by *artificial* life. Perhaps you refer to the new techniques in robotic prosthesis, but that is scarcely something that interests us here."

The reporter switched tactics. "Your assistant has refused our information crew access to your laboratories, Dr. Holland. What is it that you are trying to conceal from the citizens of Earth?"

"Absolutely nothing," said David, spreading his hands. "We have no secrets here, I assure you—apart from those natural se-

crets that as yet have not surrendered to our research techniques. At this moment the staff is not here to answer your
questions—after all, I am only the administrator. Please, come
back tomorrow and we will show you anything and everything
you want to see."

The reporter paused briefly, listening to her inner voice. Her
eyes moved to the senator, who had been standing by during
her inquisition. His eyes twinkled, the smile apparently in permanent position.

The girl nodded, looked back to David. "Without limita-
tion, Doctor?"

"No limits. We just ask that you limit the crowd so that
nothing fragile is broken in the crush."

"Ten hundred hours, Doctor. We'll have a full crew waiting."

Holland nodded his acquiescence. "We'll be here first, to
welcome you."

The girl turned away again, suddenly silent, obviously cut off
from her audience. The senator cleared his throat, capturing
the attention again.

"Well, Doctor, everything here seems to be well in hand, I
suppose I may as well run along home and get some sleep. It
looks as though tomorrow will prove to be a busy day for all of
us, so good night."

He bobbed his head once and then was gone, the lobby emp-
tying as his people and the reporter followed. Even the cameramen gave off their snooping as they received orders, and rushed
off at the end of the pack. In a moment only the Hollands and
Nathan remained.

David stared toward the now-vacant entrance, most of the
cars gone from the lawn. At least two remained, however, transport for the team of sherlocks. He glanced toward his office,
where the door was ajar, and saw someone at his desk, obviously working hard. He wondered if they had searched his
drawers and his personal files as yet. Not that they would find
anything incriminating, but the invasion of his privacy rankled,
made him feel sour.

"Well. It's started, David. We always knew that it would someday happen."

Janice lifted a hand, the fabric of her gown drifting gently with the movement. She seemed strangely out of place in the setting, dressed as usual in her favorite blue. She seemed more a courtesan, the creamy lines of her body visible in sudden surges as her dress shifted its hanging lines with each gesture.

"But nothing terrible has happened yet, has it?" she said. "Here I had myself nicely worked up for disaster, but they haven't done anything to us. To this point I must confess my disappointment."

Suddenly she sagged, Holland reaching out to grab her a moment before Nathan could react. Together they helped her to a leather sofa, David sitting beside her as she stretched out.

"I'm all right," she said, forcing a smile. "But I am very tired, David. Call a car and take me home, please."

Letermeister's sedan had vanished. David pushed into his own office, his look of rage enough to still the objection rising in the man behind his desk. As Holland stared the man slowly rose, then moved out of the way. Then he decided to step out of the room.

Using the communicator, Holland summoned a private car, then went back to Janice. A few minutes later he supported her as they walked down the steps, her weight heavy against his arm. They entered the car and rose from the grounds, the building soon lost in the darkness covering the park area.

Only David saw the security car that had been hovering overhead while they were inside, after following them from Government Center. Now it broke free to accompany them home.

SEVEN

The woman was not unattractive beneath the grime that coated her features, although it was necessary for Clay to look twice to be sure. Her hair was braided in the male fashion and wound tight into a knot on top of her head. Her body lines were not the lush fullness at the moment so popular on both Earth and Karyllia, but for all of their slimness promised a certain grace and suppleness.

Clay stifled his first exclamation as he recognized her; he glanced sideways to see if the other agent had done the same. But Martin showed no sign of recognition as he stared in obvious surprise at his prize package. Almost immediately the woman groaned, reaching up with the back of her hand to touch the queen-sized lump that had sprouted on her forehead.

She yelped at the contact, her eyes flying open as she yanked her hand away . . . and saw the two agents standing over her. "Holy . . ."

Her first sound was a croak as she recognized Martin's robes; she squinted against the noon sun and shielded her eyes with her hand as she stared up at him. The older agent went to his beast and returned with his canteen, kneeling. He cupped water into his hand and let her drink from it, then stood again.

"Well, madam?" His voice was sardonic, showing none of the kindness of his actions. "What brings a woman alone to travel this road of bandits?"

"Ahhhhh! Thank y', Holy, thank y'!"

She bobbed her head, wiping her mouth before answering as she tried to sit up; she couldn't make it until Clay offered his hand for support. Wincing again, she pulled herself to her feet, leaning against the younger man a moment until she found her balance. Her weight was no more than a child's—but her hand was gripping his wrist in a hold strong enough to bring pain.

She knew that Clay had recognized her.

Her eyes, however, were on Martin as she made her explanation, her voice now softer than the first gasped word—and less grating than it had been during the street confrontation.

"I travel to Turok's village, Holy—home of my father's house. I am a new widow, and my husband's family are all dead in the last plague. Lacking a protector, his creditors seized all of his property, leaving me penniless. I have only what I could bear away from our house on my person before they came with the warders to throw me out."

Martin nodded in interest rather than sympathy.

"It was enough to buy that miserable beast and this filthy robe, but no more. I thank y' again, Holy. You saved my worthless life. But I've nothing left with which to reward you . . . except m'self."

Martin waved a hand. "No reward is necessary, woman. Those who serve the Eternal Light are selfless by nature and generous in deed. What is your name?"

"Garlan, Holy." She hung her head as though in shame.

"Your father—he still lives in the village?"

She shrugged, the gesture eloquent. "I do not know, Holy. But where else can I go? I'm not woman enough to attract a decent man . . . I've been spurned by some almost as good as you."

"No doubt," he said. He glanced at Clay, slipping into Standard. "A convincing story, quite possibly the truth. In any event we seem to be in for company on the last of our ride—we go to the same village."

That news brought Clay around to stare sharply at the woman again. He had been debating the advisability of telling the other man that this was not their first meeting with her, but now decided to hold his silence. But there were questions he would ask at the first opportunity to speak to her away from

his companion. And considering her chosen occupation, he saw
little reason to be gentle in pressing his queries.

Was this second encounter only coincidence? After the dis-
closures of Peter Stone, Clay found it hard to give credence to
the possibility.

"Are you fit to travel?" demanded Martin of the woman. She
glanced toward the hakyar, and Clay thought that she winced.

"I'll keep m' seat, Holy."

"Then let's ride. I want to reach the village while we still
have the Light to guide us."

He whistled and clapped his cupped hands, the hakyar looking up. A repeat of the signal, and all of the beasts ambled toward them, including those of the dead bandits. A double
handclap brought them to their knees so that the three could
mount.

Clay fastened his belt tightly, secretly pleased to see that the
woman used one, too. It was satisfying to know that even a native need not be expert in the handling of the treacherous
balance. Then he reflected that being a woman in a male-
dominated society, she probably had had little chance to practice the male arts.

Although she was fast enough when it came to cutting a
purse. . . . What other proficiencies did she have with the
thieves' weaponry?

"What about them?" he asked, indicating the corpses that
were already attracting interested insects and small flesh eaters.

"Leave them," said Martin. "They died without the Light,
so let Darkness claim them."

He kicked his beast into rising and then into moving out,
once again taking the lead. The other two hakyar fell behind in
single file, the native woman in the middle. Clay studied her
without her knowledge as she leaned back in the saddle, her
eyes closing against the brightness of the sun. Occasionally she
winced as the pain jarred anew; then her features relaxed as she
fell into a doze, soothed by the rocking gait of her beast. After
a time Clay did likewise.

The afternoon passed slowly, Clay wishing for the watch he had left on the space station, although long hours of hypnotic impression at Academy had set his subconscious clock to an accuracy as great. Garlan slept for more than an hour, coming awake instantly only a moment after Clay had opened his eyes. She blinked, staring ahead at Martin; then looked around at Clay. She touched her beast and it slowed, dropping back to take up position beside Clay's mount.

"You show proficiency with the sword, sir." It was not necessary to show him the same respect demanded by Martin's priestly robes. "What is your name?"

Clay told her, and she shaped the sound, making it almost two syllables. "Clahyh; a most peculiar name. You come not from Ahd-Abbor. Where is your home?"

"In the mountains," he said, giving the simple explanation of every agent.

"Um. And that is where you joined up with the wearers of the white robes?" She nodded. "There are many mountain men in their service. They must be very powerful in your valleys to demand such obedience."

"They serve the Light."

"And the Light serves them," she said, the sarcasm suddenly biting. But as she said it she glanced ahead to see if Martin-as-priest had heard. Her relief was obvious when he did not turn around.

"You have no faith?" asked Clay.

"Faith enough in what my own hand can accomplish," she returned, holding it up with muscle flexed.

"You should visit the Temple of Eternal Light."

"Oh, I've been there," she replied. "I've seen the free food for the belly and the free place out of the cold wind at night. When you're hungry it's a fair enough exchange, listenin' to the sanctimony."

"You must admit that it's more than the Sanctum will do. The priests of Darkness do nothing but bleed the populace, take their last crusts, take their houses when it suits them. What is right in that?"

"I never said anything was." She jerked her head toward Martin. "Him—puff-breast there. What is his name?" When Clay repeated it, she shaped it with her tongue. "Mah-tan. Another man of the mountains, I suppose."

"As a fact, we come from the same valley."

"Why did you all leave? Too cold for decent farming?"

"To serve the Light."

She glanced at him quickly, as though suspecting that he was pulling her leg; then spat to the other side. A moment later she dug her heels into the sides of her hakyar, the beast shambling ahead to take up its center position in the file again.

They had moved into hills high enough to make a noticeable change in the ambient air temperature, Clay's heavy underclothing no longer so uncomfortable. Now they crested a barren rock ridge, and saw below a long narrow valley, marked through the middle by the silver stripe of a stream. The valley was wooded at this end, but halfway along turned into open fields.

The road dropped sharply over the ridge and soon they were in the forest, the trees tall and leafy, blocking the sun from the trail. The world seemed absolutely still except for the sound of the hakyar's pads moving through the leaf mold that now covered the road. Clay kept glancing nervously to either side, a feeling of something impending tightening the muscles across his shoulders. There should have been the sound of insects, the call of birds, the chittering of small animals; but there was nothing at all.

He looked ahead, saw that both Garlan and Martin were alert. But the older agent did nothing to encourage his beast to move faster—and then Clay was sure he saw movement from the corner of his eye. He turned quickly, his hand going to his sword rather than to one of his concealed weapons in deference to the presence of the native woman. But there was nothing.

He convinced himself that it had been an animal, and after a few hundred meters managed to relax slightly. There was no feeling of intelligence watching, but the atmosphere of the forest was chilling, foreboding. After a time he felt clammy, and touched his forehead to find a cold sweat beading. He shivered as he wiped it away.

He touched the sword again, recalling now the strange sensation that had come over him as he used it to draw native blood. Awkward in appearance, it balanced well to his hand, the product of a Terran machine shop rather than a native forge. The steel was far stronger than any native manufacture, singing in his hand as it cut through air and flesh alike. It had been a good feeling, he realized now, feeling embarrassment at the touch of blood lust.

And then they were coming out of the woods without incident and moving through the cultivated fields. Another half hour brought them to the village, built on top of a knoll to take advantage of the natural drainage.

A naked child playing in the dust saw them first; its outcry brought the attention of several older children no more dressed, who immediately scattered to bring the word to the rest of the villagers. As the hakyar climbed the little hill Clay studied the half-hundred mud-walled, thatched-roofed huts that were scattered across the knoll in an arrangement without order. Then they were among the huts and surrounded by perhaps three times as many adults as there were houses.

Martin brought the procession to a halt, looking around as Clay saw a blackened circle to one side, in the midst of which were half a dozen stubbled remains of more huts. Then the village headman was coming from his house, a graybeard who leaned heavily on his staff of office for support. He stumped through his people, pushing to where he could look up into Martin's face.

"Holy? We have seen your face before."

"At last harvest, Turok. Does everything go well with your lands and your people?"

"The tax collector was here a ten-days or so ago, but he left us enough to plant new crops, perhaps even to feed our bellies through the winter."

Martin nodded. "It is good. Are we welcome?"

"So long as Turok lives, Holy, the priests of the Eternal Light will always be welcome."

"It is good," said Martin again, signaling his beast to kneel. Clay and Garlan followed suit, the two agents staggering slightly as they adjusted to solid ground again, fighting for balance. The youth noted with jealousy that the native woman had no problem.

"We have brought one of your daughters with us," said the older agent now, and Turok squinted, looking first at Clay.

"Huh? Who?" He moved closer to Garlan, peering into her face. "She wears the robes of a city man—a woman! I know her not."

"My father was Haslak," said Garlan as the headman shook his head, obviously disgusted. "He sold me at the age of eight to a caravan master, who sold me again as a bride in Ahd-Abbor. Now my husband is dead."

"Haslak, huh!" Turok shrugged. "Stupid man. He sold his children, even the males, and had no one to take care of him when he got sick. He's long time dead."

He turned away, waving a limp hand. "She can stay while she's with you, Holy. Now we will have feast tonight!"

He clapped his hands and a half-grown youth came running. Despite the great difference in age, the family resemblance was marked.

"Tell Mura to give his house to the Holy, then take a strong young dak to Tessuk to butcher."

"Thank you, Turok," said Martin. "You are a good man."

Turok grunted, "Only good, only good," then shambled off, leaving the agents to ponder the meaning of his words.

Clay watched him disappear, then glanced swiftly at Garlan. The native's expression was unreadable, the news of her father's death not even registering. Of course, she had been sold into slavery as a child, so there was no reason for her to have affection for the man. At the moment, however, she gave no indication that her future seemed bleak.

"What will happen to her now?" he asked, slipping into Standard. Martin shrugged.

"If she's lucky, a bandit will capture her and make her a wife. Or a slave; it makes little difference."

"And if unlucky?" pressed the youth.

"When her money runs out and she has no property left to barter for food, she'll starve."

The thought was chilling. Clay watched as Garlan unloaded her hakyar of a meager pack and disappeared between two of the huts. Knowing her so briefly, he was willing to bet that she would never starve. Or end as a slave to some bandit chieftain.

The youth returned from Turok's errand. "Mura's house is yours now, Holy," he said.

Martin nodded. "Help my servant with the baggage, boy."

He strode off without looking to see that his command was obeyed. Apparently Mura had been the hapless host of the priests before, for Martin stooped to enter the second-best hut on the knoll top. When Clay followed a moment later, he found the older agent stretched out on a bed of springy fur-covered boughs.

"There's vermin enough for both of us, Holland, but you may as well get used to it now. Your own stink will help some, for we strangers aren't as tasty to the bugs as the natives. Better prepare yourself for itching, though."

He sighed, kicking off his boots and closing his eyes. While Clay was still arranging their baggage a soft snore came from his drooping mouth.

There were half a dozen of the beds scattered about the open interior of the hut, but nothing else in the way of furnishings. The floor was hard-packed dirt, with a fire pit in its center that Clay knew was used for heating only; all cooking was done over the community fires in front of Turok's hut. The stripped saplings that made up the framework of the buildings sprouted limb stubs in various positions, most of which were used as hooks for hanging the meager possessions of the villagers.

The only light in the room was that which filtered through the door opening, although there were several small stone lamps of the same type Clay had seen in the temple resting about the floor. Most of them seemed filled with rancid fat

that stank even now when they were not lit. There was a hole
in the peak of the roof to let out the smoke of the fire; rain was
kept out by means of a flap that could be pulled over the hole.
Choke or soak seemed to be the only alternatives.

There was a snuffling noise outside the hut, spinning Clay
around in sudden alert apprehension. The noise continued, following the curve of the wall, and then a shoat poked its snout
through the door, sniffing the alien odor of the agents. It
pushed in, curious.

"Go on! Scat!"

Clay picked up the nearest object, a half-woven sandal, and
shied it at the animal. The shoat squealed, spinning around to
bang against the door frame as it fled to safety. The walls shuddered, dislodging a shower of dust and straw from the cracks.

"There'll be others."

Clay spun, to see Martin with both eyes opened. The agent
scratched beneath his arm.

"This is probably his house—his, along with the rest of
Mura's livestock. At night they'll be ambling home, so you'll
have to make the most of it. You can throw out the human inhabitants of the place, but you can't dislodge the animals."

"I thought the place smelled like a stable."

"No—like a low-culture agricultural habitat. The separation
of the two functions comes much higher on the cultural ladder.
I'll wager the temple is the only structure in Ahd-Abbor to
keep the animals out of the community quarters."

He closed his eyes again, and almost immediately the soft
snoring resumed. Clay finished his small task of housekeeping
and looked longingly toward the other beds. After so many
hours in the saddle his musculature and bones begged for relaxation, and the fur-covered cots looked far more comfortable
than the pallet at the temple.

Then Martin dug at another worrisome itch on his side, not
opening his eyes. The older agent snorted, and turned on his
side, presenting Clay with a view of his back. The youth opted
against following his example and ducked out of the entrance.

The adult population of the village had disappeared once the upset of the agents' arrival was finished. Clay walked through several of the huts without seeing anyone other than the same naked child. Then he looked down the knoll into a field of ripened grain and saw a flash of dark color. A moment later there was another as several of the villagers moved through the stalks, tending to their roots.

Clay stopped where he was to watch. Beyond the field was a wild orchard, and between the two wandered a small stream. The setting seemed ideally pastoral as he spotted several of the daks meandering between the fruit trees, eating falls from the ground.

But this was not a picture, and beneath the surface appearance life was far from ideal. Turok was a crippled graybeard, probably the oldest man in the village; but Clay knew it was doubtful that Turok had seen as many as forty winters. Even discounting the astronomical infant mortality, the average life span for those who survived their fifth birthday was only twenty-seven Standard years.

Karyllia in no way could be considered a paradise. The people were ill-housed, overworked, underfed—and oppressed by the priests of the Sanctum. The villagers made up 98 per cent of the planet's population, drawn together in close clan relationships. As headman, Turok was both all-powerful and the abject slave of his fellows; so long as he could protect them and feed them in time of famine, he could be absolute ruler. Let him fail once, however, even in a small way, and a blunt instrument would crush his skull to make way for a new Turok.

Clay found it difficult at the moment to relate these deprived ciphers with the ancestors of his own race. Yet man on Earth had followed a clearly marked trail toward civilization and toward the stars. Human history on Earth was barely ten millennia old, but in that time men had clawed their way from the first crude agricultural settlement to the mastery of stellar space.

Karyllia was several thousand years along that same path already . . . but left to themselves, would they break the planet-bonds as the Earthmen had done? Why force hundreds of generations to suffer needlessly, when the older and wiser race could offer secret guidance that would short-cut those thousands of years that otherwise lay before them. Was there a universal law proclaiming that each planet must experience the long path of error and suffering for itself, making the same mistakes, learning the lessons of a history already ancient on Earth?

It didn't seem right that such be the case. There were only three known intelligences in this region of the galaxy, all of them following parallel lines of evolution that had brought them at last to the form of man. It was staggering to the imagination that such be no more than coincidence.

The men of one planet could not crossbreed with those of the others, but the relationship drawing them together was unmistakable to any eye that could look and see. One superior intelligent form, taking shape everywhere that advanced life was possible. It was natural, it was the order of the universe.

Clay could not understand the hatred of the Humanity Firsters, the force that claimed superiority for Earth simply because its branch had been fortunate enough to evolve to culture a few thousand years earlier than Karyllia and Locane. They were misguided zealots to be so blind . . . never realizing that he was a zealot himself.

He stirred, an aching in his neck muscles telling him that he had been standing in one position too long. He rubbed his neck and swiveled his head several times to loosen the vertebrae, then interlaced his fingers to crack the knuckles. He knew from his weariness that it was time to follow Martin's example and sleep away the remaining hours of the afternoon.

He turned to retrace his path through the huts, a winding way that nearly doubled the distance to the house of the unfortunate Mura. He rounded the hut that was but one removed from Turok's—and stopped. A small figure was slipping furtively along the same path, taking shelter in the lee of each wall.

Garlan started to glance back, and Clay flattened himself

against the nearest wall. When he looked cautiously around the curvature again, she was gone.

He followed, catching sight of her again as she repeated the same sly movements. Then she was at the hut presently shared by the off-worlders, and ducking slightly to slip through the door. Something glinted in her hand . . . something black, like the thieves' knife she knew so well . . .

EIGHT

The demonstrations began the next morning, a score of pickets already in place when the Hollands arrived before 0730. This was no spontaneous affair of homemade boards and hasty anger; the Firsters were well prepared for the confrontation. Several of the signs contained crawl messages while at least two others featured fifteen-second animated cartoons.

"How long have they been here, David?" asked his wife. "It's only the first morning!"

"As soon as there was an audience, I suppose."

He was relieved to see a security car parked on the lawn before the main entrance, and two guards standing before the door. Their company of last night was still trailing them, however, and as their aircar settled to the ground it took up the same hovering position as before. David wondered if Janice had seen it.

The instant the door opened the sound washed over them from the pickets and their signs, deafening for such a limited group. Janice shuddered and hurried up the steps into the building as David followed, turning on the top step to look down at the protestors.

"Monster makers!" shouted one woman, shaking her fist.

"No androids on Earth!" boomed one of the signs. "No androids on Earth!"

"Criminals! Declassification is too good for you!"

"Put 'em to death with their monsters!"

"Traitors!"

"No androids on Earth!"

Holland hurried through the door then, the sound mercifully

cutting off as the heavy wooden panel closed. He saw Nathan, waiting, along with his personal secretary, Jenny, here an hour before her usual time.

"That has been going on since dawn," said Nathan.

"The day is early yet," said David. "There'll be more of them as soon as the cameras arrive. 'No androids on Earth'—do you suppose it's all right to have them on other planets, even the moon?"

"Certainly not on the Guided Worlds," said the technician, smiling weakly. "I think that one's a mistake that will be caught as soon as someone in authority shows. Usually the key phrases are more carefully constructed."

"The sherlock in your office asked me to arrange quarters for a dozen auditors, David," said Jenny. "The staff lounge is the only room big enough. The fellows have already cleared out the tables and the couches."

"I doubt that anyone will find much time to relax during the sweep," said Holland. "Has everyone arrived?"

"Waiting for you in the lab," said Nathan.

"Then we may as well go down and see what can be done to keep things running during this upset."

The crowd out front grew larger when several buses arrived, discharging hundreds of passengers and departing immediately, only to return again with another contingent as Senator Wiley's limousine settled gracefully to the ground. By that time Holland had requested additional security guards, after fighting his way through a surly duty officer finally to reach the district commandant. He felt drained when he finally turned away from the communicator and closed his eyes, letting the robot sensors in his chair set a soft relaxing vibration.

"Ah, Doctor! Resting?"

He opened them to see the senator standing in the doorway, a cameraman crouched against the wall of the cramped office quarters to get both of them into his focus. As always, Wiley seemed pleased with the way things were going—and with himself.

"Scarcely resting, sir. Is there something you wish to see me about personally?"

"Ah, no, Doctor—don't stand." He held up one hand. "No, I think I'll be returning to my office now. After all, the duties of government do not stop merely because of one investigation."

He started to leave, turned back. "Oh, there is one thing, Doctor. My committee is scheduling a hearing on this matter in five days. You'll be Commanded to appear, of course. In fact, your entire staff will be Commanded to appear."

With that he was gone, leaving Holland to stare moodily at the space he had occupied. The cameraman scurried away.

That was the first day.

The next days were little different. The crowd outside stabilized at nearly a thousand. Three-quarters of the bodies were drones, swept from the nearest barracks and rewarded with an extra ration of happy juice. They showed their enthusiasm vocally, loud enough to penetrate the sound conditioning of the building. It was a low muted roar that frequently increased in volume, but never seemed to diminish.

Auditors, reporters, and cameramen came and went while the staff continued to perform their duties in the lab. On the third day Nathan came to Holland early in the morning, worried.

"David, ten eighty-three is showing signs of prematurity."

"How old is she?" Odd numbers in the series were female; even, male.

"Thirty-five weeks, four days," replied the technician. "The computer recommends that we let her come to full term immediately. Several of the late-terms are showing signs of emotional distress, David."

"Did you run a trace on ten eighty-three?"

"Back to conception. The record shows double O balance all the way, so it is not the system."

As in natural-host birthing, the gestation period of the developing fetuses was approximately nine months; but also as in natural patterns, the time was not exact; it could vary by a normal three to five days. Occasionally, however, a child would come to term in considerably less than normal. More rarely a fetus would cling to its artificial womb for as much as forty-five weeks.

One of the side studies of the program was to try and determine the cause of such variations. To this moment there was a great deal of data but not a single conclusion as the computers kept demanding additional information.

The following day Nathan was back with another problem.

"David, the entire staff has been Commanded to appear at Wiley's hearing—everyone! We have no cadre to stay on watch over the life support systems, and right now it looks as though ten eighty-three is going to decide to be born right about the moment the gavel drops."

Holland sighed and tried to call the senator. He found himself unable to penetrate the outermost barricade, a supercilious assistant demanding his name and identity number, as though he were not now familiar to every citizen on the planet. When David complied, the information was recorded in a manner implying both boredom and contempt.

He put an urgent summons to Letermeister, the Commissioner of Science coming on the screen in a matter of minutes.

"It's still an official government program, Charles," he finished, after relating the nature of Nathan's plight. "At least, until the sledgehammers begin their smashing."

"Of course, David. Even a Senate committee cannot force a halt to an official function before malfeasance has been proven. At the moment he hasn't even filed formal charges. I'll speak directly to the President if Wiley refuses my personal call."

"Janice heard a report that says he is favoring the Reformationists," said Holland.

"Nonsense!" Letermeister's outrage was the natural shield of a man who had spent his entire life in appointive service, as had the President. "What good would it do him, facing ten years mandatory retirement from public position when his term expires?"

The head of the government was a position largely ceremonial, as it had been for most of the past century. Occasionally a strong-willed man came to the office, however, and during his six-year term took effective control of the machinery that operated every aspect of the social structure of the planet. Even a nominally weak president still commanded the security forces and the Navy.

"Incidentally," said Letermeister, "I too have been Commanded to appear. At my convenience, of course. Should I refuse, David?"

"Is there anything to gain or lose by taking either position?"

"I suppose not." The commissioner sighed. "I really did not expect to retire so soon, David. I find the very thought of inactivity appalling. I've no idea how I shall ever manage to survive."

"Perhaps we can find mutual interests to stir our intellects, Charles. Unless I'm reassigned to managing one of the southern sewage reclamation districts or desalination plants. That would be even worse."

"It is a possibility," said Letermeister, soberly, ending the conversation.

Not since the first confrontation with Wiley four days earlier had anyone connected with the Project mentioned the possibility of the ultimate penalty: Declassification.

It was too frightening to contemplate.

An altered Order of Commandment appeared the next day, permitting the necessary number of technicians to stay with the life support systems. Holland noted that it was signed by a minor member of the committee, rather than by Wiley himself. He feared that it was an indication of the man's pettiness.

That night Janice produced a half-liter of brandy from the same mysterious hoard that guarded the coffee. They shared the intoxicant, although even with the alcohol filtering into his bloodstream David felt remarkably sober. They went to bed early and held each other close through the night.

And then it was the day and the hour appointed for the hearing before Senator Wiley's committee. It was a chill October morning when they reached the roof pavilion to find their air-car already waiting. David shivered as he handed Janice into the car, the cold cutting into his mouth as he took a breath. And then the brief exposure to the elements was ended, the interior of the car conditioned to comfort level. At Government Center it was unnecessary to expose their skin during the transfer to the building.

Senate hearings were normally held in limited quarters, but the interest in this had caused a transfer to a fair-sized auditorium. The audience was surprisingly large, several hundred people; David recognized many of them as being high in government service. There were even a dozen other senators, evidence of the high-level interest in the proceedings. Every seat was filled, most of them with citizens above even yellow rank.

The summoned witnesses were sequestered before their appearances in a room apart. Letermeister was not among them, although there were several that David did not recognize. They were strangers to Janice and the staff as well, sitting apart from the pariahs of the Project.

"Prosecution supporters," Janice suggested.

"This isn't a trial," said her husband, stiffly. "It's only a formal enquiry."

"Please, darling." Pained, she placed one hand over his. "Don't belabor the obvious."

The preliminaries were concluding now, the last member of the panel settling into his place. Wiley was neither first nor last to arrive, smiling genially at his fellows and at the audience when he did come in. As always, he was surrounded by aides and assistants, far more than accompanied any of the other senators.

The focus switched to the table occupied by the Speaker for the Committee, a young man with legal training and political ambitions. He cleared his throat and stood, looking at the panel assembled, although he was obviously aware of the camera following his every movement.

"Senators." He bobbed his head once in greeting; there were nine on the panel, seven women and one other man besides Wiley. "We wish to begin these proceedings by laying groundwork for the inquiries to follow. The subject is one of general

anathema to the citizens of Earth today as it has been historically."

He paused for emphasis, aware that his audience was locked
on every word. Just those with access to the citizen's channel
were watching, of course; the only time the drone entertainments were interrupted was to address polemics keyed to emotional responses.

"As a result," continued the Speaker, "there is limited
knowledge of the subject matter among the general citizenry.
Therefore, I call as my first witness Dr. Lathen Tarlfin, a geneticist, and an expert who can fill in the background for us before we proceed with this enquiry into the forbidden android
research."

There was a stir through the audience as the outrageous
word was finally mentioned, although David Holland and his
staff had grown so used to the recorded pejorations of the hired
demonstrators the past several days that the word had lost all
shock value. In the Project itself, of course, the word was never
mentioned, even obliquely. David tried to recall the last time it
had been voiced, and decided that he hadn't heard it since the
day thirty years ago when Letermeister had tapped him to be
administrator of the new Project.

At the time Janice was brought in to be team leader, the position held by Nathan for the past three years. She had already
established her reputation as a researcher into the medical as-
pects of human mutation, and it was a simple matter for her to
make the adjustment to the new focus.

Working closely with the Commissioner of Science, they had
recruited the staff for the Project, most of them young and en-
thusiastic workers chosen because they were not bound to the
accepted areas of scientific development. Later most of them
had advanced to other programs—apart from Janice and David
Holland, only Letermeister remained as a link to the Project's
beginnings. Talented, the early staff had quickly risen through
the ranks and colors of citizenship, earning positions of
influence throughout the scientific community on Earth.

Nathan had come in seven or eight years ago, quickly showing that he was as good as any of his predecessors. In the long-term program Holland had already tagged the younger man to be Janice's successor, and eventually perhaps even his own. Certainly Nathan's administrative abilities were as strong as his technician's qualifications.

David had not heard from most of the former Project workers in the years since their replacement. Now he wondered if perhaps Wiley's source lay in that direction. Perhaps one of them had undergone a personality change, now sought only personal advancement or power. Janice's testing had weeded out the weaker personalities at the beginning, but in time anyone could change.

At the moment he hoped that his speculation was correct. He certainly did not want to think that the source could be someone still connected with the Project. Holland had few remaining illusions, but he wanted to think that he could trust the people that were as close to him as though they were his own family.

As the Speaker called out the name one of the strangers in the witness room stood, adjusting his tunic and unconsciously running a hand over the back of his hair. Holland and the others watched with interest as a marshal opened the door and the witness walked out to be picked up by the camera, immediately appearing on the screen larger than life. He took the witness chair and was sworn in, then crossed his knees and laced his fingers together.

"Dr. Tarlfin, you are a geneticist connected with the Research Institute for Geriatric Diseases?"

"Yes." He nodded.

"As such, Doctor, you are familiar with gene and chromosome construction techniques?"

"Yes, I am. Genetic engineering is basic to the study of human diseases."

"What exactly, Doctor, is an android?"

"Well." He rubbed an ear, his professorial manner obvious as he prepared to lecture. "Classically, an android is a synthetic human being, created from chemicals. The term comes from the Greek, *androeidēs*, meaning manlike. The term first gained wide circulation during the twentieth century, in fantastic romances."

"Yes, well, that's quite interesting, Doctor. As the term is understood today, *what* is an android?"

The witness spread his hands, smiling. "A human being born without benefit of natural parents."

"I see. The human reproductive system is in no way involved?"

"None whatsoever."

"Well, then, how is an android brought to life?"

The legs shifted, crossed again. "It is a chemical process, involving the most extremely detailed genetic construction. Starting with the basic nucleotides, you proceed to build the genes, the chromosomes, the ovum to be fertilized. It is not necessary to actually duplicate the spermatozoa, although the early techniques did so. The male chromosomes can be directly applied to the ovum. The fertilized ovum is then raised in a host environment through the normal period of gestation."

He smiled again. "This is of course a simplification of a most complicated process, but in essence it covers the process followed."

"Then successful androids have been created before?"

"Oh yes—during the twenty-first century. The most successful experiments were carried out in the Chinoamerican Coalition before the Great Dictatorship was toppled, when it was feared that great armies of mindless automatons would overwhelm the free world nations."

"Yes, well, we all know, Doctor, that further experiments into android creation were outlawed by the Compact. Is such an army possible—androids built to serve specialized functions only?"

"It is possible, yes."

"Thank you, Doctor." The Speaker looked at the committee. "Are there any questions, Senators?"

A woman gestured. "Dr. Tarlfin, how may an android be distinguished from a person born naturally?"

"Well, it would be a difficult matter to establish. One possibility would be to do a gene comparison against the supposed true parents. If even one gene could be located in the offspring that could not be matched against either of the parent-pair, then the parenthood claim is false."

"But how can the android be identified as artificial?" the woman insisted.

"There is no way, madam."

"Then anyone could be android?"

"If the construction program could be proven to have been carried on over a long enough period, yes."

There was a moment's silence as the impact of that statement sank in. Holland was watching Wiley's reaction, the senator making a signal to another of the panel. That woman indicated a question and was given the floor.

"Why would anyone consider an android desirable?"

Wiley nodded as the witness again shifted his position, quite obviously aware that he was the center of attention for the whole classified world.

"Under perfect conditions, apart from those of specialized uses, an android would be an ideal realized. The creation would suffer none of the failings of normal-born humans, for there would be none of the genetic faults to which all normal people are heirs. He would be better in every way, in intelligence, in ability, in health."

"You are speaking of superman," said the woman.

"Of *homo superior*, certainly. It was recognized at the time of the Compact that normal births could never compete with the laboratory product. That is why androids were outlawed."

"Can androids breed true?" asked another, without waiting for recognition.

"I don't know. I know of no reason why not, but it certainly would not be necessary. There is no need for parenthood when life can be created in the laboratory—or the factory."

"Are there any more questions, Senators?" The Speaker looked at each in turn. "Thank you, Doctor. You may step down. I now call Dr. David Holland to the stand."

Janice caught his hand again, squeezing hard. "David, it's not too late to change your mind . . ."

He shook his head. "No. There's no point to it. The whole story has to come out, and this is the best place for it to happen. They'll have to listen."

He held to her fingers as he rose in answer to the marshal's summons, Janice clinging as long as she could. Then he was moving through the door and onto the stage of the auditorium, blinking at the change in light level. One of the cameramen scurried close to focus on him as he walked to the witness stand and turned to face the Speaker.

"Dr. Holland, you are aware that this is an official enquiry of the World Senate, and that you are presently within the field of equipment that is testing your emotional and physical reactions with a 95 per cent probability, given your psychological profile and pathology, of detecting any falsehoods or evasions of the questions?"

The words came out in one long breath, leaving the Speaker to gulp in replacement air as David nodded his head.

"I am."

"Then be seated, please." He rubbed his thumb and forefinger against his chin for several seconds before fixing David with his stare. Even then he did not speak, the tension rising, until another twenty seconds had passed.

"Dr. Holland, it has been said that you are now and have been for a period of many years engaged in illegal research into the production of androids. Is there any truth to that statement?"

"There are half-truths in the statement."

"Sir?" The Speaker seemed astonished. "Half-truths? What do you mean? I ask you again, and directly—are you engaged in android research and construction?"

Holland swallowed, closing his eyes for the briefest of intervals. Then he looked straight at his inquisitor.

"I am, sir."

There was instant bedlam throughout the auditorium, as though the audience had come to hear the worst but expected him to lie his way out of it. Wiley was on his feet now, smiling sardonically as the uproar momentarily drowned out the rest of David's statement. Holland was also on his feet, leaning forward to grip the rail around the witness box, shouting.

"You must listen! Listen to me! No one has asked *why* we did it! You must understand!"

The audience bedlam was easing considerably, but now Holland's words were falling flat before they could even touch the ears of the committee members. Only the Speaker could hear him.

"You may as well save your voice, Doctor." He beckoned several of the guards, and as soon as they were within the cone of the silence generator, said, "Arrest him."

NINE

The hut swallowed the Karyllian woman, leaving Clay to cast quick glances around to see if anyone else was audience to what was happening. There was a raucous cry from elsewhere in the village as a tethered egg-layer reached the end of its leather rope, flapping wings in dismay; Clay could see one of the blue-skinned dogs lazing in the sun, snout upon its fore-paws. Then the shoat came snuffling again between Mura's house and its nearest neighbor. But there was no sign of human life nearer than the distant fields.

He crossed the space between the huts in a crouching run, coming up against the wall of the hut to listen. After a few seconds he made out a soft air-gulping snore that could only be Martin. It came again at regular intervals; to this point the other Earthman was all right.

Clay bent to release a gas grenade from his heel, then thought better of it. He slipped the thumbnail grenade into his robes, his hand then moving to the hilt of the thieves' blade taken from Garlan in the city. The Karyllian sword had been laid aside as soon as the agents' baggage was moved into the hut.

He went into a crouch again, preparing to rush through the door—when suddenly Garlan was coming out. For an instant her attention remained back inside, time enough for Clay to throw his knife-bearing hand around her middle and lift her into the air.

Instantly his arms were filled with forty kilos of fighting hell-cat as the native woman raked at him with her nails, her heels raining hard-edged sandal blows to his shins and cracking his kneecap. Clay yelped once in pain and fury as her elbows pummeled his midriff repeatedly, and then she was trying to claw his eyes and attempting to sink her teeth into the unprotected hollow of his throat.

The cords in his neck stood out as Clay gasped with the effort of trying to control the fury of the little female. Although his mass was twice Garlan's, her strength seemed nearly as great as his own as she continued to twist and turn in his grasp. All of his concentration held to keeping her still, his hand locked now about the wrist holding the knife as she cracked her head against his chin, bringing stars to his eyes. Before Clay could recover she brought her foot up in a rear kick between his legs, almost reaching his unprotected groin.

He locked his thighs about her foot, crouching automatically as her fingers caught in his hair and yanked, pain stabbing all of the way through his braid and into a saucer-sized circle of the skin covering the top of his skull. Her fingers twined into the greasy strands and yanked again while she did her best to catch his nose in her teeth, ready to grind it into sausage. She missed, but her forehead banged painfully against his chin, driving his lower lip against his own teeth and bringing the taste of blood to his mouth.

"Stop it!" he hissed, still trying to use the strength of his arms to control her. It was a futile effort.

"Pig!" hissed Garlan in gutter dialect. "Off-world carrion scum! For touching me, you'll die!"

Seconds later the sense of her words penetrated the concentration and Clay went taut in surprise. He stared down at the native's squirming head, wondering if he had heard wrong. But the meaning of her words was unmistakable, leaving him only one thing to do.

He threw himself forward, putting as much energy into the action as he could. They fell together, Clay landing heavily atop the little native and knocking the breath from her. Then he planted one knee in her back, twisting her arm painfully.

"Be still!" he said, angry. "I'll break it off!"

She called him obscenities in dialects that were new to his ears, the meaning unmistakable by the tone, and made a tentative try at twisting free. But she was securely pinned, and she subsided, recognizing a condition unchangeable by physical exertion.

"Stop!" warned Clay after the tirade had continued for the best part of a minute. "Stop the nonsense now!"

"Kill me!" she retorted. "Go ahead, scum! Kill me with my own knife like the dishonorable carrion you are!"

"A thief talks of honor?" he said.

"Thieving is an honorable profession—unlike yours, which skulks behind the robes of a false god."

"Then you're not very good at it. This makes twice now you've been caught. What were you doing in the hut?"

As he said it, he glanced toward the entrance. The hanging over the door was hooked back to let in the daylight, and he could see Martin still stretched out on the bed. It seemed incredible that the uproar had not awakened the man, and now Clay was sure that the woman had killed him—but as he watched, Martin stretched and turned over to a new position, never opening his eyes.

Now Clay realized that the entire battle had been carried out in whispers, his voice hoarse with the effort as each had tried not to arouse other interest. They had succeeded; apart from the once-sleeping dog, which was now on its feet, watching them closely, none of the villagers had heard. The shoat had been frightened away, leaving the arena clear. Fortunately none of the other huts opened on this particular space.

"Who are you?" Clay demanded.

"An honest thief," retorted the woman, "looking for something that belongs to me!"

"This?" He held the knife in front of her eyes, which glittered dangerously. But she did not answer. Clay eased the pressure on her arm, shifting his weight so that his knee no longer pressed so heavily against her spine.

"Give me your word there will be no more nonsense and I'll let you up."

Garlan bit her lip but again did not answer. After perhaps twenty seconds Clay released her and stood up. She looked more than ever like a small child as, after a few more seconds, she rolled over, rubbing the twisted wrist and flexing the injured shoulder. She continued to stare up as the many pains she had inflicted on Clay's body began to score their toll in separately identifiable complaints.

"Who are you?" he asked again. "What are you doing here?"

"You have my name," she said, wincing as she sat up. "I told you the truth."

"Your name I'll believe—the rest of it, no. You're no thief."

"I won my blade in the alleyways and marketplace!" she said, insulted. "Fool!"

"Twice caught, you call me fool?" Clay shook his head. "Unless you wanted to be caught . . ."

There was no answer to that, and he asked, "You took something else of value from me that night. Where is it?"

Garlan seemed puzzled by the charge, although the look was fleeting, her face quickly returning to impassiveness. She shook her head.

"I took only your purse, which you had back fast enough."

"More," he insisted, fumbling in his robes for the new filters that had been given him in Ahd-Abbor. The little electronic plugs were sheathed in magnetized metal that clung tightly together. "These."

Garlan stared at the plugs as Clay held them in his fingers, again shaking her head. "No, I took nothing but your purse. Do you think a thief has time to search every pocket and fold? On a dead man or a drunk, but not someone on his feet and moving, no matter how stupid he may be."

The taunt stung; only Martin's alertness had made Clay aware of his loss. He had never felt the woman's fleeting fingers, had barely been conscious of the brushing contact that gave her opportunity. But it was obvious that lies and deceit were the normal pattern of existence to her; he filed her denial under pending enquiries that could wait for their answers; there were more important questions to be asked.

"What do you know of off-worlders?"

Again the blank look, although Clay could have sworn that a fleeting emotion had shone from her eyes. This time, though, she did not deny her knowledge as Clay grew impatient.

"You spoke the word!" he said, sharply.

"I know curses in a dozen tongues, pig!" she countered. "You misheard. I know not 'fwulders.' It sounds sickening—I trust it is a loathsome disease that will make your flesh rot and your fingers and toes and sex fall off!"

Clay surrendered, but returned to his first question. "What were you doing in the hut? What were you looking for? This time the truth!"

"I wanted my blade," she said. "It is me . . . mine. My soul is locked in it . . . without it I die. If it breaks, except in honor, I die."

"That is why you are here?"

She nodded, eagerly. "Yes!"

"But how did you know we were coming this way?" he asked, his voice suddenly softer in tone, even though they had been talking quietly. "You were waiting for us, not behind us."

"I followed you from Ahd-Abbor until I saw you take the western road. Once away from the settled country this is the first village. I cut across the fields and got ahead of you—would have been here first except for the accursed bandits!"

Her story was plausible; it was possible that she had skulked about the temple, looking for an opportunity to regain her weapon. There was no control over the natives who came to take advantage of the Light's charity, and Clay's movements had been in no way restricted. Dressed in nondescript and keeping her distance, Garlan could easily have passed for just another proselyte.

Only the single misspoken word showed that she was something more, but how to get the truth from her, lacking the mind probe or drugs?

"Your soul, eh?" Clay studied the knife, tossing it loosely in his hand. "I think I'll keep it, woman—that way I'll know exactly where you are."

He was ready for her lunge, meeting her with a stiff arm that sent her tumbling backward in a tangled somersault. Before she could recover he had placed the blade across a small rock, his foot balanced across the arch.

"Stop or I'll break it now!" he warned as she came to her feet, ready to rush him again. "There'll be no honor in this, Garlan!"

Hatred burned fierce in her eyes, but she stopped, time suspended for an instant, her hands out for the attack. Then she spat to one side and turned, moving swiftly between the huts.

Clay was astonished by the sudden change, and by the time he retrieved the blade and slipped it within his robes to follow her, Garlan had disappeared.

Clay stopped, frustrated; she could have vanished into any of the huts, or slipped completely away from the village. He started to bend, to enter the nearest hut, then realized the foolishness of the idea. Apart from disturbing the villagers, the outcry of his invasion would warn her long before he could come upon the right place, giving her plenty of opportunity to escape again.

He returned to Mura's hut to find Martin still sleeping soundly, his rest undisturbed. Shaking his head at the man's ability to sleep, Clay pulled the night flap over the door, securing all three ties on each side. He started to sit down on the nearest unoccupied bed, which was against the wall—and changed his mind in mid-squat. The hut walls were flimsy, no protection against the quick thrust of a sword. Instead, he moved to a cot that was more than a meter away from the wall, settling at last.

Another mystery had been injected into an already confused situation: who was Garlan? For a moment the idea that she might be another agent—or at least a Terran—had appealed to him, but examination now forced him to reject that conclusion. She must be a native of Karyllia; a woman that small in stature could never have passed the entrance qualifications to be admitted to Academy. She couldn't be more than 120 centimeters or so.

Could she somehow be an agent of the Reformationists? If so, how could she have arrived on the planet? This area was under routine surveillance and space flight was strictly controlled. Only Academy vessels were admitted to the stellar systems holding the Guided Worlds. If on the other hand she had been recruited on the planet, then someone had broken the Compact. In Clay's knowledge, such simply did not occur. The Compact was the strongest set of laws ever to have ruled Earth. There might be crimes against property and person, but the Compact was above such considerations. It was a moral force without the seedings of religion. The idea that it could be broken was unthinkable.

He closed his eyes, resting, although sleep was still far away. And then Martin was touching his shoulder, shaking him awake.

"Huh? What—" Clay started to come off the bed, reaching for Garlan's knife. Then he made out the older agent's form in the gloom and relaxed, yawning and cracking his jaw. He did the same with his knuckles. He arched his back—and then became aware of a score or more places where his bedmates had decided to sample his flesh and his blood. He made a face, scratching, as Martin reached into his own robes, bringing out a dead something between thumb and forefinger. The agent made a face of his own, dropping it into the fire pit.

"Time to be moving, Holland." He indicated the roof hole, where dusk was gathering over the sky. "Our hosts will be ready to hoorah us as soon as the last light is gone."

Clay rubbed his chin, feeling the stubble of his beard, growing again under hormone treatments now that he had stopped using depilatories. The natives shaved to a man, and a beardless man was unknown, quite probably would have been a pariah. Tomorrow he would have to hack again with the naked razor, a task he hated.

He wished he could wash, but such was not to be unless they came upon a brook or lake, until they reached the temple in Des-Abbor, the seaport that was their last scheduled port of call on this mission. Oh, the natives knew enough to scrub the dirt from their faces and hands, at least in this region; but there were no bathing cults in the area.

As Clay pulled on his boots, Martin dug for another visitor, disposing of it in the same manner as the last.

"The thing I hate most is the delousing when we check into the nearest temple. You were bathed while you were unconscious, Holland, so you have no idea of the pleasures in store."

He started on the ties and by the time Clay joined him at the door Martin had the night flap pulled back. They went out to where a red glow could be seen dancing off the walls of the nearer huts, coming from the cooking pits. The strong odor of scorched meat came from the same direction, and Clay's stomach flip-flopped, even though he had been aware of hunger since awakening.

They made their way to the space before Turok's hut, where the women of the village were preparing the feast. The dak was slowly turning on a spit, turned by a half-grown girl who had to strain to reach the handle when it was at its highest point. Unfortunately no attention had been given to the handle when the beast was run through; it was off balance just enough so that it was heaviest at that time and required a great deal of effort to turn.

There were other, smaller spits over the fires as well; the menu would not be limited to the single meat dish. Other girls were stirring great clay pots, the sweat from the fires drenching their simple shifts. The women bossed them constantly, barking orders that frequently contradicted one another.

Turok came out of his hut, grunting and scratching and still leaning heavily on his staff. He moved toward a circular arena a dozen meters across that had been scraped out in the dirt in the middle of the central space. A bed had been brought out for him, and now he lowered himself to it heavily, muttering curses at the weakness of his own body as he at last managed to cross his legs.

Furs were brought out now and folded into pillows, then placed on the ground before either end of the bed. Martin moved to one of them without invitation, lowering himself in the same fashion as Turok but without complaint. Clay took the other. Despite his height advantage over the natives, when he looked up he was still a head lower than Turok.

Other men of the village joined the circle now, sitting on the bare ground. Several of the women appeared with jugs, offered to Turok first. The headman swallowed deeply, then spat, spraying both Clay and Martin with his spittle.

"Ahhhhhh! The warm death is good tonight, Holy. It goes straight to the heart."

Clay found a jug pressed into his hands and immediately smelled sour beer. His stomach protested again, and for a moment he thought that he was going to be sick. But the immunizations injected while he was on the space station worked, and he forced himself to drink sparingly as he watched Martin draw as deeply as Turok.

Once the first round of drinking was done, the jugs passed from neighbor to neighbor until drained, it was time to begin serving the food. The honor of serving the men was obviously too important for the girls who had done the work of preparing the various plates. Great wooden trenchers were brought first to Turok, a tiny slice cut for him to gobble down and nod approvingly; then the meat made the rounds. A woven grass plate was shoved into Clay's hands, greasy from former uses. Before he could protest it was filled with dak and other unidentifiable flesh, and then a large roast tuber was plunked in the center of the mess.

"Eat up, Holland!" said Martin, jovially. He was already digging his fingers into the mess. "This is Karyllian hospitality at its best!"

Clay ate slowly, every time his fingers became empty a jug of beer shoved into them from his right side. It was impolitic as well as impolite to pass without drinking, and so the beer continued to filter into his system, the level of alcohol in his bloodstream growing so high that the immunization was unable to prevent intoxication. His head was beginning to buzz and he was growing dizzy; on Earth he had never known intoxicants, which were frowned upon although not forbidden by the Compact.

As the feast progressed there was entertainment, although it was difficult to make out the near-grown wrestlers who took the circle first with the only illumination that which came from the cooking fires. It was impossible for Clay to determine which player was which, although from their groans as they rolled about the circle they were entering into the spirit of the occasion with the greatest of enthusiasms. Then one was jumping up, aiming a vicious kick at the other's head, and presumably declared the winner. The other pulled himself to his feet and they staggered from the circle together, the audience hooting with appreciation.

The center of the ring was taken next by a pair of sword wielders, Clay at first interested as the native blades slashed about with alarming swiftness. The metal caught the fire glow, gleaming dully red. Then he saw blood spout from a severed artery and knew that this was no game.

He looked at Martin, but the older agent seemed interested only in his jug. Clay started to say something to him, but the injured man lost his footing at that moment, tumbling forward to end nearly in Clay's lap. The victor helped him from the circle, and that section of the entertainment was finished.

Now several of the men in the circle were getting up to leave momentarily, an idea that appealed to Clay after the quantity of beer he had drunk. He got up to follow, but saw them returning, having left for a reason different from the one he supposed. They had gone no farther than the ring of women who were standing a dozen meters behind the men, and now each was dragging a giggling conquest back to the circle.

"Ah, yes." Martin wiped his mouth as he spoke in Standard, his humor high. "We've had what passes for the wine, Holland, and what passes for the song. Now it's time for the native version of, you must forgive the expression, women."

"Have they no modesty?" Clay asked, horrified. This had never been mentioned in the tapes at Academy.

"None that we would recognize. Choose, lad—but take my

advice and try to find one with a really repulsive stink. The chances are her bug infestation will be less than that of her mates."

"Not me! Oh no!"

"You must, or Turok will be grievously insulted."

"What about you?" he countered. "You're not picking."

"Ah, but I'm exempt. While I was here last year I managed to convince good Turok that certain priests are sworn to special vows. They can lie with women only in the great temple and only at the most propitious times. The old fellow is impressed by any priesthood; he believed me."

Although the term would not have been familiar to him, Clay's education was highly Puritan in its morals. He stared at the mating going on about him, wondering in panic how he could escape. Martin was chuckling as he watched the youth's obvious discomfort, and offered no help.

Then a small figure was standing beside him, slight in build but attractive in a gown that certainly had never seen loom in this village. It was city stuff, fine and expensive, clinging to the lines of her figure. Her fine hair had been combed out until it seemed to billow in the soft light of the sinking fires, floating about her shoulders and half covering her arms.

Her hand touched his shoulder, and she smiled—and with further shock, Clay recognized Garlan. After a few seconds he scrambled to his feet, tongue-tied.

She laughed, her voice musically soft as she reached up to touch his face. There was none of the harsh thief now, nor of the hellcat of this afternoon. Clay stared down at her sharply delineated cheekbones, saw the way nostrils cleansed of grime flared over full red lips. There was a gentle odor as well, perfume rather than unwashed body, the scent tantalizingly familiar yet almost exotic in its strangeness.

"Who *are* you?" he demanded, catching her wrists and exerting cruel pressure with his thumbs. The native woman winced but did not try to draw away as her perfume seemed to exercise a hypnotic effect on the youth. Gradually the pressure relaxed.

"I am Garlan," she said. "Daughter of Haslak of Turok's village, member of the Thieves' Guild, exile from my home. I am a woman alone in the world who must make her way as best she can."

"No." Clay shook his head, conscious that this woman was beautiful even if alien. "You're more, much more—that dress! Where did you get it?"

"It was one of the few miserable pieces I managed to rescue from the greed of my dead husband's creditors."

"No street woman nor merchant's wife ever owned a dress like that! It belongs to a courtesan, to the consort of a war lord. *What* are you, Garlan?"

Her words had been whispered, heard no farther than Clay's ears. Now she looked at Martin and saw that the effects of the beer had finally overcome him. He leaned back against Turok's bed, his hands hanging straight at his sides and his head drooping while a snore issued from his throat.

"I am Garlan," she said again, "woman of Karyllia. I am going to save your life, Earthman . . ."

TEN

David Holland stared at the approaching security guards, tears of frustration stinging the corners of his eyes as his words fell unheard a scant meter away. This was not the way it was supposed to be—by the Compact they even now claimed to honor, they were supposed to hear him out, listen to *why* he had committed his supposed great crime.

Janice had been right; she said they wouldn't listen, and they were following her predicted pattern to the final degree. The guards were at either side of him now, one clamping something about his wrist—and then a shock stabbed through his body, causing his hair to stand with electricity, his muscles to tense into tremor. That effect lasted no more than a second, but when it left he felt as though he were encased in ice. The guard tugged at his wrist and he moved out of the box in movements that were stiff and jerky.

Holland tried to turn his head, intending to look toward Wiley, but independent movement was impossible. His body was completely under the control of the guard and whatever the instrument was that was attached to his wrist. From the corner of his eye he saw that several of the senators were standing, but Wiley wasn't in his field of vision. Then even that much was gone as he reached a door and was led out. As the door started to close behind him he thought frantically of his wife, still in the witness room. What were they doing to her, to the others?

The next twenty minutes were nightmare as he continued under the control of the guard's device. They moved through endless corridors and elevators, and finally Holland was pushed through a door. There the device was removed, and he staggered as his muscles were released from control. Before he could recover, he heard the door click locked behind him.

He spun around, staggering still as his body adjusted to free control again, to see an absolutely blank door panel, devoid of any control mechanism. A sudden shout made him spin to his right: a small screen built into the wall was showing the public entertainment channel, at the moment a gory scene of battle with slashing swords and great splashes of blood spattering through the air. Wincing, he moved forward to silence the screen . . . but like the door, there was no available control system.

He was in a tiny room. A narrow bed occupied most of the room, a single chair locked to the floor at its foot. A table shelf was partially slid into the wall below the screen, while a single narrow locker, also built-in, offered storage space. Opposite the room's door was a small 'fresher, a single shower stall that could be entered only by sidling around the stool. A lavatory could be folded down from the wall over the stool.

The room was quite the smallest Holland had ever seen, although it was as large as any blue cubby. Even married blues did not receive double the space allotment, although their quarters had to be large enough to contain a bed big enough for two and an extra chair and locker. David had visited the quarters of his technicians several times over the years—they at least had room enough to turn around in, and shelf space for prized personal possessions.

This was obviously a detention center, considering the lack of controls on door and screen. He winced as he glanced at the latter again, the noise pounding in waves of increasing passion calculated to stimulate the emotions of the watching drones and blues. It was succeeding only in giving him a headache.

"Shut it off, please!" he begged, knowing that someone must be listening. But the request was ignored. The screen was mounted flush with the wall, making it impossible to cover with his tunic.

He sank onto the edge of the bed, hopelessness dulling his

emotions. There was a vacant sensation in the back of his throat as he lay back, the bed adjusting to him; it read the tension in his body and began a gentle massage as Holland felt very much like crying. He knew the response was anything but mature, but at the moment maturity seemed an attribute without value.

Where was Janice? Nathan? The rest of the staff? What was happening at the Project? Was his the only arrest, or had they all been taken?

There were no answers to any of the questions without contact with the outside world. And at this moment he was sealed off completely from such contact. He closed his eyes, recognizing that excitement was useless, and that questioning the unknowable was pointless.

Sleep did not come. His eyes opened; his thoughts were too chaotic to permit relaxation and none of the control techniques he tried were effective. The sound of the public channel nagged incessantly at his ear, even when he turned on his side away from it. The wall served as a baffle, bouncing the echoes back in undiminished volume. There was no way to escape the onslaught, lacking the filters that had been designed for the agents on Karyllia as protection against the sonics of the native religion.

Karyllia. He thought of his son for the first time in days. Clay must be in action by now—how much had Peter Stone found it necessary to reveal to the boy? The knowledge of the race's deterioration was held to only a few at the highest level, but now that Wiley had forced the issue it would have to be made public. The crisis was real, was the reason for the Project, could no longer be hidden. Perhaps it should never have been hidden.

Time passed with excruciating slowness as Holland waited for something, anything, to happen. The entertainments on the public channel shifted periodically, timed to the normal attention span of the intended audience. Unable to find release in the wanted sleep, he at last began to watch, wondering what minds had created this confusion in the first place. The technicians assigned to producing the stories must be shell-hardened to normal sensitivities. It was obvious that most of the actors were drawn from the ranks of the blue, although their work earned them special privileges that gave them position just below the yellow.

Holland consulted his watch regularly, saw that most of the entertainments lasted no more than thirty minutes. It was two hours past noon; had they forgotten him entirely? Despite his dark mood, his body knew hunger.

There was an interruption then, the door sliding open to reveal a gloomy-faced young man no older than the Speaker of the Committee who had assured his political future this morning. The man carried a portfolio, which he placed in his lap as he took the single chair in the room, the door sliding shut behind him. There had been no sign of anyone else in the corridor outside.

"I am Pel Maslan, Dr. Holland. I have been appointed your public defender."

Holland sat up. "My wife?" he demanded.

Maslan shrugged. "I really don't know anything more than what was presented at the hearing this morning, Doctor. Is your wife a fellow conspirator?"

"No!" He tried to control his anger. "Neither of us are conspirators, sir—not in the sense you mean."

"Of course." His mouth pursed. "However, she has been associated with you for a long time, has she not?"

Holland nodded. "She has."

"The public charges against you have just been read—I have a copy here for you." He opened his portfolio and took out a sheaf of legal documents. Holland accepted them dully, glancing briefly at the first page.

"These were prepared quickly enough."

Once more came the other's shrug. "I really have nothing to do with those matters, Doctor." It was obvious that he was not pleased with his position. There was no glory on this side of the Holland affair.

Holland stared at the man a moment, the silence growing

awkward, until at last Maslan shifted uncomfortably. He swallowed and cleared his throat.

"It is not necessary that there be a trial," he said. "Further publicity may be avoided, further unpleasantness, if you simply plead guilty to the charges as broadcast."

"And if I do?"

"Well, the matter ends there, of course. The decision will be made on the basis of your plea."

"And what happens to me then?"

Maslan spread his hands. "That depends on the tribune, of course. I'm sure you were aware of the penalties when you began your illegal research."

The defender obviously was avoiding unpleasantness by refusing to give them voice. Holland felt a sour humor convulse his stomach as he stared the man into fidgeting with the handle of the portfolio. At last he shook his head.

"I want my story told. I want the citizens to understand why I did what I did—why it was necessary for the Project to follow the paths that carried us into android research. I still have the right to be heard, do I not?"

"Very well, Dr. Holland." The portfolio produced a recorder. "Please state all relevant facts so that I may prepare an official plea for clemency."

Holland gathered his thoughts for a moment, eyes closed in pain as he recalled the circumstances which led Charles Letermeister thirty years ago to establish the android project in violation of all of Earth's laws. The matter seemed so serious and yet so frightening in its public implications that the President of the time agreed that secrecy was necessary. Even then Janice had argued that the citizens should be told what was happening, but she was overruled by the psychometricians opted to the original study.

The government expert had been wrong in making it sound to those listening this morning as though android construction was an easy matter. Many difficulties made it seem as though they were following blind trails, perhaps purposely laid by the world's leaders at the time when androids were first outlawed.

Yet androids had been successfully created then, and the laws of nature had not changed.

It took seven years before the staff at last found the right trail, and another three before the first android infant was born a success. There had been many failures during those three years, and many others that were at best partial successes, before a completely viable child was produced with every evidence of adherence to the ideal.

In the twenty years since there had been other failures, although the rate had grown smaller over the course as they learned the mistakes they had made in the beginning, and knew as much what errors to avoid. No more than 10 per cent of the children tested out ideal, although there was none of the recession of intelligence in the android births that could be charted in human crèches over the same period of time. Whatever recessive gene was responsible for the deterioration had not been duplicated in the android banks.

As yet the oldest of the androids were still years away from the social norm or marriage, but according to every test Holland's technicians had been able to devise, they could breed true—they would breed true. The problem now was to set up programs to increase greatly the number of androids born—from one a week to one a minute. Letermeister had been planning the finances of the stepped-up need . . .

The problem now . . .

After perhaps twenty minutes Holland's words ran dry, and his mouth closed; he stared at the young defender as though expecting some visible transformation with an understanding of the crisis facing the race. He was disappointed; Maslan blinked once, and stirred.

"Is that all, Doctor?"

"Is that *all?*" repeated Holland, incredulous. "Haven't you been listening? Haven't you heard a word I said?"

"Of course. It is a very pretty fantasy, Doctor, but of course you don't really expect anyone to believe such a paranoid nightmare. The race most certainly is *not* regressing—look at the progress we are making in the stars. Historically the trend of

the human race is ever upward. Society has most certainly not
come to a standstill, is most certainly not deterioriating around
us now. Not unless you have a different concept of deterioration than I do."

"But it is!" he insisted. "You can't see it from the middle,
any more than the Romans of the fifth, sixth, or seventh centuries could see that darkness was falling about them. But it
happened—it *is* happening, now!"

"Well, I shall have to be one with the Romans, Doctor."
Maslan stood. "I shall come again as soon as I hear the results
of the plea, although I fear it will do little good to prepare for
this trial. Public anger is very great, and any judge who might
be assigned has to be swayed by the emotionalism of the people. Still, it will be an exercise in technique, if nothing more.
Good day, Doctor."

"Wait!" said David, coming to his feet. "I must see the
Commissioner of Science!"

"I will certainly relay your request."

The door opened then, proving that the room was under
constant monitoring, and Maslan was gone. The panel closed
again quickly before Holland could move toward it, and before
he caught more than a glimpse of the bare corridor wall opposite. He sank down onto the bed again, lost in his own gloom.

Some time later the door slid open again, without warning,
a blue guard standing there with a robot waiter. The man lifted
a tray from the receptacle, there not being room enough for the
waiter to maneuver around the furniture.

"Pull out the table, happy!" the guard ordered. "Whatcha
waitin' for?"

Holland did as he was commanded, forced once again to
stare at the screen. As the guard set the tray before him, he
asked, "Can't you shut that thing off? Or at least turn it to the
citizen's channel?"

"Can't do that, happy," the blue said, cheerfully, dropping
into the chair. It was obvious that he was going to keep the
prisoner company during the meal. "Never shuts off, goes all
night. Hey! 'Arko's Circus'—that's wunna my fav'rites!"

As Holland worked at his ration he was forced to listen to a running story line of the entertainment. "Y'see, Doc Arko—hey, he's a doc like you! Well, anyways, he has this thing for pretty slicks, but they gotta be young, see. He pretends he loves 'em, but what he really wants to do is take 'em home an' do 'em in so's he c'n cook 'em! He's wunna them watcha call cannobballs, an' he likes to eat pretty slicks best of all. There, he's doin' it t' her now! Yeah, slice that slickie, make her scream, Doc! Hey, I wunn't min' tastin' some o' that myself, huh!"

Holland looked at his plate and felt suddenly ill; he pushed it away. By lowering his eyes he could avoid the scene on the screen, but there was no way to cut out the sound. And the effects were graphic; the girl's scream was still dying away.

"Don't they ever, ah, catch the villain?" he asked.

"Naw! What they wanna do that for? All the fun's in watchin 'im slice those slickies. They catch ol' Arko there won't be no more fun left."

He spotted the abandoned tray and unwound himself from about the chair, not too disappointed that the entertainment was over for the moment. There would always be another episode and another dismemberment to cheer him up again.

Once again Holland was alone, the questions he had intended to ask the guard driven out by the grisly horror on the screen. Another just as bloody had taken its place, however, and he lay down on the bed again, turning toward the wall so that he at least wouldn't have to look at what was transpiring on the screen. The sound was bad enough.

With only his thoughts to keep him company, the evening passed as painfully slow as the afternoon, his hunger returning after an hour or so to remind him that he had not finished his meal. It would undoubtedly be a long time until breakfast. He was at last at the point of dozing off when the door clicked again, and he turned over to see Letermeister.

"Charles!" He scrambled to his feet, hands out to greet his friend. "It took you long enough to get here."

Letermeister touched hands lightly, dropping into the chair

as though his age had suddenly caught up with him. His eyes closed in momentary pain.

"The President asked for my resignation tonight, David. He agreed to let me withhold it a few hours, to make this my last official function. He can wait no longer, however; the pressure from the Reformationists is the greatest ever. Wiley is demanding that the President call a general election."

"Janice? Where is she?"

"Arrested. In a room a few doors down."

"Nathan? The others?"

"All arrested, David." He sighed. "They turned the drones loose in the Project. Everything is sacked."

"The fetuses? The embryos?"

"Aborted, all of them. There were no medical technicians on hand, not that it would have done any good. The late-terms that could survive were . . . murdered."

Holland slumped, wincing with pain; thirty-five lives lost. Some would not have survived in any circumstance, because there had recently been problems that caused Janice's suggestion to tear down the network and rebuild it from scratch. They had been trying to eliminate the last possibilities of error in the system, planning for the day when they could move into full-scale activity.

All dead. He felt every loss completely.

"I'll be seeing Janice when I leave you, David. I'll see them all. It's the least I can do . . . the last I can do."

"Don't tell her about the destruction," said Holland. "Keep that much from her."

Letermeister nodded. "There's a witch hunt going on, David. They're trying to track down the androids, uncover their hiding places."

"Most of them are only children. They don't know that they are android."

"It makes no difference. It's mostly the blues, so far, although they've swept the barracks in a few of the districts, turning the drones loose as well. They have the smell of blood . . . several have been caught already, those they could prove came from the Project. The Firsters have the list and they've been broadcasting it ever since the morning."

"Thank Wiley for that, I suppose."

Letermeister sat straighter. "Wiley is only a tool, David. The forces are greater, perhaps even natural. He thinks he sees the way to quick power, but he is really only responding to the demands of the populace."

"They don't want to hear the truth." He told the other about the visit from the defender. Letermeister nodded.

"The world is in for another time of madness, David. I very much fear that the Bad Years are with us again. I at least can retire . . ."

It was not necessary to finish the thought. The commissioner stood, offered his hands.

"I'm very sorry that I brought you into this, David. I won't see you again after this, I'm afraid. So this must be good-by."

"Good—" David bit his lip, unable to finish the word. "Will I see Janice at the trial?"

Letermeister shook his head. "No, David. You'll never see her again."

He turned to face the door, which quickly opened. Holland watched as his closest friend stepped out without looking back and started away. The panel closed quickly, leaving Holland with the noise of the public channel and his own private grief.

But not for himself; his grief was for the unborn children murdered this day, for the others who would be destroyed while still in childhood. It was a terrible burden, one that weighed most heavily on his conscience.

Yet they wouldn't find them all. From the beginning the possibility of discovery before they were ready had been known and planned for. As many of the infants as possible were smuggled into life, their identities buried deep in false records, their lives swapped for natural stillbirths without the knowledge of the supposed parents. There were several hundred of them by now—not enough; not by any means enough. But the time of insanity would pass again, would have to pass again, and their chance would come.

He spent a restless night, sleeping in fitful dozes that left him heavy with fatigue when a blue brought breakfast in the morning. Despite his hunger, he picked listlessly at his food, then followed the guard's advice and used the facilities of the 'fresher. Apparently it was considered essential for prisoners to be clean for their trials.

The public defender returned an hour later, Pel Maslan still holding to his portfolio. He did not bother to sit down.

"They are ready for your trial," he said.

"My plea for clemency?"

"Rejected."

Holland stood, shrugging. "Then there's no real point to this affair, is there?"

"You may still plead guilty," said Maslan.

"But it won't affect the results." The other shook his head. "Then I'll make them earn their citizens' allowance by doing the whole job."

Two of the guards appeared at the door and Maslan stepped out. Holland started to follow, when one of the guards approached with a wrist device. He tried to fend the man off.

"That isn't necessary."

"Regulations, happy," replied the guard, snapping the control in place. He activated it, and Holland was dragged forth, once again an automaton.

The trial was to be held on this floor, which saved him a measure of agony; when the control was removed he found himself standing in a witness box in a small court, the tribune already behind the bench. The only other person in the room was Maslan.

"David Holland." The judge peered down from nearsighted eyes. "You have heard the charges as broadcast. How do you plead?"

"Not guilty," he said, standing, although it wasn't necessary. The judge looked at Maslan.

"The evidence of your statement at the enquiry yesterday contradicts your plea. Do you now have counterproof evidence to indicate that the original statement was false?"

Maslan shook his head. "No, mercy, we do not."

"What about my statement?" cried Holland. "What about my reasons for doing what had to be done? You must listen— the world must listen!"

"A trial is a private matter between the accused and the government," said the judge. "No outside witness may be privy to what occurs in these chambers, under the terms of the Compact. Extenuating circumstances have been adjudged not to exist in this case, David Holland; you have already admitted to the truth of the charges. Therefore there can only be one verdict.

"Guilty," he said, picking up his ancient symbol of office and rapping it sharply on the little wooden block.

The ceremony done, he lay the gavel down on his bench and folded his hands. With his bristly topknot, he seemed the caricature of a petty government official, one enjoying this moment of personal power even if there were no audience to share his pleasure.

"David Holland, in the absence of extenuating circumstances, the penalty for violation of the Compact is clear and compelling. The court may in its wisdom temper the administration of justice by easing the degree of punishment, but in this case sees no reason for leniency. Because of your crimes against the Compact and the citizens of the world, you are hereby Declassified to the ranks of the unclassified, and will be transported from this district at the first opportune moment."

With the pronouncement the shield that separated the bench from the witness box went opaque, the first intimation that Holland had had of its existence. He turned to Maslan, but the defender was busy with his portfolio again, rearranging the few papers so that he would not have to meet Holland's gaze.

David started to speak, then thought better of it. What use to force an issue on an obviously unwilling audience? The man was performing his own function under compulsion, so let him escape.

The door slid open and the two guards were there, the same

one advancing with the wrist control. Before the shock could stab through him once more, Holland had time for one last clear thought: triumph. He knew that they would never find all of the androids. They were too well hidden, well covered . . . particularly his own son.

Clay Holland . . . android!

ELEVEN

Clay was aware that they were beginning to attract attention from the villagers, the men in the circle staring openly. Even Turok sensed something happening and raised his besotted head, mumbling something unintelligible. Nothing like Garlan's dress had ever been seen in this village, and no woman like this one had stirred the lust urge basic in the males. The women lacked even the knowledge to dream of a fabric so fine; a stir of excitement swept around the little arena.

"Reject me," said Garlan, softly, "and Turok will take me first. When he's done, the others can have their sport."

Clay knew that his ears were flaming with embarrassment as he stared deep into the Karyllian woman's eyes. They burned with strong fires, were nothing like the eyes she had worn earlier. Was the woman a witch, able to change form and parts at will?

"What should I do?" he asked, nearly choking.

"First put your arms around me."

It was necessary to release her wrists first, Clay sure that she was laughing at him as he did so. A rage against her boldness formed deep in his chest as he complied with her instructions. He did know what to do with a woman . . . but he had never expected to be called upon to perform the social graces in so unusual a place.

Garlan was not the first female to have filled his arms, or so he reminded himself as he placed his suddenly oversize hands against her back, gathering her into an awkward embrace. There had been others, even a public woman who had taught him the final meaning of the words "male" and "female."

Why then was it disconcerting to discover that despite the wide variance in their size and physical structure, she fitted well, even comfortably, against him? His robes prevented Clay from feeling the lines of her body as they melded with his own, but her scent was stronger now in his nostrils, her grip as force-ful as it had been this afternoon when she wrapped both hands around his neck.

"Well?" She *was* laughing at him. "Kiss me."

Clay did as she ordered, his lips barely brushing hers, the pressure so light that he didn't realize her mouth was parting. He tried to pull away then, but Garlan held him close, whisper-ing into his ear. Beneath the perfume her scent was clean, and he wondered how she had managed to bathe. Then he realized that her words were further instruction.

"Tell Turok that you're taking me to your bed, Clahyh. But watch Mah-tan!"

Clay looked around the circle, the men dropping their eyes even though it would have been near impossible for him to see them staring in the dim light of the now-banked cooking fires. A few of the villagers had left the circle with their choices, al-though most had returned to their place in the group. There was giggling as many of the men busied themselves pleasing the women in an attempt to hide their new focus of interest.

Martin was still slumped in his stupor, the snore that was his trademark issuing from his gaping mouth. Clay broke free from Garlan's embrace to capture the headman's attention.

"You! Great Turok!" The old man peered from beneath heavy lids, one eye nearly closed in an obscene wink. "I choose this one for tonight. We go now to the hut."

Turok mumbled something that Clay took to be reluctant assent. The headman studied the little woman closely, how-ever, perhaps remembering and regretting his rejection of the afternoon.

Garlan's wrist was pressing against the circle of Clay's thumb and forefinger. He had the presence of mind to close the circle and pull her away from the gathering, feeling the jealous eyes of the villagers drilling deep into his back.

"Turok is planning how to take me," said Garlan as soon as they were beyond the nearest hut. "He knows now he made a mistake, and he doesn't like that. He's thinking he's been made a fool."

"What can they do?"

"Seek to avenge the insult."

"Against you?"

She laughed, stopping now to look back, as though expecting pursuit. "Against a woman? He would lose all honor. No, he will strike against you."

She started to move on through the darkness, but Clay caught her wrist, pulling her back. He again caught her arms.

"This has gone far enough!" he said. "I want some explanations, Garlan. Again I ask—who are you, and what are you?"

"We've no time for words now, Clahyh. We must move swiftly. I've two hakyar already saddled with our baggage. If we ride fast, we can be four granyar away before the Light comes back."

"No." He shook his head. "Answers now!"

"Clahyh, you must leave the village now! If Turok and his men don't kill you, Mah-tan will!"

Clay stared, uncertain for a moment that he had heard correctly. Her statement was preposterous . . . but Peter Stone had said that Martin was a probable enemy. Were the Reformationists aware of Clay's own role in this matter?

The mission was as much to determine the other agent's true loyalties as for any other reason. Still, Clay found it difficult to believe that another Earthman would have reason to *kill* him. Such things happened only on the public channel. It was doubly incredible with the warning coming from such an astonishing source.

"How do you know?" he demanded.

Garlan saw that she must humor him. "Mah-tan himself told me."

Clay felt trapped in ancient slapstick, which was currently undergoing a revival in the citizen's entertainment media. The matter was becoming more and more ludicrous, each time that

Garlan spoke her words pummeling him further with the air-filled bladder. There was no real pain for the actor, yet there was hurt that could not be ignored. But if this were slapstick, where was the audience . . . and the laughter?

He closed his eyes, concentrating on his dilemma . . . and then his ears separated a single sound from the night background, one made forever recognizable through years of field exercises on Earth. Every cadet schooling to be an agent had been caught by that sound again and again, until a special neural pathway was burned deep into the patterns of the brain. One lesson of stinging eyes and heaving belly was enough to ensure alertness during training techniques; repeated a score of times, it could never be forgotten so long as the hearing remained functioning at any near-normal level.

There was only the single soft pop as the plastic shell of the gas grenade self-destructed, but Clay reacted instinctively, dropping to the ground and pulling the native woman down with him. His hand went over her mouth for an instant while he wasted precious oxygen of his own on a single warning.

"Don't breathe!"

Then he was scrabbling away on knees and elbows, his hand still tugging her wrist and forcing her to follow as best she could. Garlan understood the significance of Clay's actions, locking her lungs and rolling with him, ignoring the damage the ground was doing to the dress. They covered perhaps ten meters and rolled against the next hut, then Clay was up in a crouching run, putting distance between them and the small cloud of death that was even now dissipating, rising into the air where it could harm no one but a chance night bird after its unsuspecting dinner.

They wove through the haphazard arrangement of huts, not stopping until they reached the edge of the village, slipping partway down the grassy verge of the knoll. Clay let himself fall back then, gasping in deep lungfuls of clean air as his eyes saw red sparks dancing from the temporary oxygen starvation.

"What is it, Clahyh?"

"Gas." He looked toward her, saw that Garlan was on her

hands and knees, watching the direction from which they had just come. He sensed the perplexed expression, her features ghostly pale as the bright moon started to appear over the ring of hills to the east.

"Poison that moves through the air," he said now. "You can't see it and once you smell it, you're dead."

The gas in the grenades carried by agents in the field was not the regurgitant used against the unsuspecting cadets. It killed silently and swiftly, the invisible cloud catching the air in the lungs and the voice in the throat. Even while it choked it was filtering through the pores, traveling through the bloodstream to freeze the heart in a convulsive seizure during the final instant of consciousness.

She stiffened, reading the fright in his voice. "What devil's death is this?"

"It had to be Martin," he said, resigned. "It could be no one else."

"I warned you!" said Garlan, excited. "Mah-tan was only pretending to be drunk, Clahyh. Give me my knife—my soul must have the taste of his blood!"

"We've got to get away. Where are the hakyar?"

"We can't run now, Clahyh. It's too late for escape. We must kill Mah-tan before he can summon help from the villagers. Give me my knife!"

The hatred was sharp in her voice, seemed almost an aura visible about her body. On her knees now, she held out both hands to him, beseeching.

"My knife!"

He felt within his robe and touched the hilt of the obsidian blade, caressing it briefly. Then he brought the thieves' badge out, reluctantly handing it across to her. By no means did he feel that he could trust her—but at the moment there seemed to be no one else but Garlan to trust.

"Your bootlace," she said. "I need it."

It was clear that the native woman was far more familiar with this situation than Clay, even with his training for the bizarre realities of alien planets. He bent to do as she said, the top of his boot flapping wide open as he unwound the leather thong. She took it, measured a short piece, and cut it with her knife, giving him back the lesser part.

"Use this to tie the top of your boot so it doesn't hinder your movements."

He did as instructed, and while still bending, released three of the gas grenades from his own cache. After a second thought he added three of the explosives from the other heel, their cases brittle enough to enable differentiation from the gas grenades without his having to look. If Martin was going to violate the Compact, it was only fair that Clay should have the same weapons available.

At the moment, however, this was still an affair of silence, the explosives only a last resort. He started to touch Garlan's shoulder to show that he was ready, and saw that the native woman was bunching her skirt about her waist, tying it out of the way with the remains of his bootlace. Her movements now unencumbered, she nodded to him, and they moved together back among the huts.

Where was Martin? Clay remembered his decision to give up the search for Garlan this afternoon, futile with so many open hiding places; it was much worse now with darkness covering the huts, making them impenetrable. No lamps were lit, all of the villagers either around the arena or lost in lust that needed no lighting.

Only one thing made their task easier: Martin must also be searching for them, to finish what he had failed to do with the gas attack.

Clay wished for a glowtorch in his pocket, but such items were restricted from the Guided Worlds as indicating too high a degree of alien technology should they be discovered. It was impossible to conceal a functioning atomic light in the presence of the natives, and so the agents were forbidden its comforts even when locked away in their private fortresses, lest one should accidentally be distributed in the wrong place. They were forced to get along with the illumination available at this technological stage of Karyllia's development, bad as it was. Nor could they suddenly introduce incandescent lamps or even arc lighting; electricity was still many technological generations in the future.

The bright moon made it easier to slip between the huts, but made it more difficult for them to hide in the shadows that were now sharply delineated across the ground. At first Clay found himself confused in their present location; then his natural sense of place let him mark out the direction of Mura's hut, to their right.

"Where are the hakyar?" he asked, whispering.

Garlan looked at his face, saw no intent to flee; her sharp retort evaporated. "On the other side of the village, at the bottom of the hill."

"Any danger they'll be discovered?"

"No. They're tethered well away from the others."

He nodded, satisfied, and started toward the center of the village. But before they had covered half the distance there was a sudden outcry, voices raised in anger and outrage.

"Mah-tan!" said Garlan, softly. "He's told the others."

There was a great deal of drunken cursing, Turok's bellow prominent in the uproar. Clay froze, wondering again if it would not be best to retreat now, deal with Martin later. He could return to Ahd-Abbor, summon help from the temple.

But Garlan was moving ahead, toward the commotion. Angry, Clay thought nasty words to describe the woman's idiocy. But he knew he couldn't leave her to her own devices; as competent as she had proven herself, she was no match against the strength of the village men.

He moved after her, caught her as she crouched by the hut nearest to the arena. Clay touched her shoulder, watching the scene of total confusion.

Turok was on his feet, shouting curses, while Martin was moving around the circle, kicking the village men into movement. But they were too drunk to respond as he wanted, staggering when they tried to stand, many of them falling over or slowly folding back to the ground. The agent was cursing himself, in Standard and in the gutter dialect of the district, his words no more effective than his blows.

"Turok!" he shouted. "What useless dak-beasts do you hide in the skins of your men?"

The insult was terrible, but the response was no greater than before. The last of the villagers sat down, his legs out straight before him, his hands between his thighs. He stared up at the angry Earthman, giggling foolishly. Then in slow motion he fell over on his side, snoring.

With a final kick at the hapless man, Martin strode from the arena into the darkness.

There was nothing to fear from the villagers. Clay turned his attention to the problem of Martin—and heard a muffled cursing in his inner ear as the agent stumbled against something in darkness and activated his communicator. There were other sounds, soft rustlings and a sudden intake of breath that made him think the other to be in one of the huts. Clay touched his own skull, tracing the shape of the implant but careful not to activate the transmitter as another sharp curse came, Martin bumping into something else.

There were fifty huts, but only one logical choice as Martin's location. Clay moved swiftly toward Mura's hut, covering the distance in less than a minute, fearful that Martin would come out again. But the sounds continued in the communicator, as though the other were searching for something. Clay's pack, already removed by Garlan?

"Holland, where *is* it?"

Clay stiffened as the question came sharp in his ear. But it became obvious that Martin was only talking to himself, lamenting his failure to locate whatever *it* was. If he suspected Clay of responsibility for removing it, most likely it was some item of off-world technology. What could he have smuggled from the temple?

Mura's hut was before him, the thatched roof silvery in the bright moonlight. Clay stared, crouching, his fingers touching the ground as he planned his next move. Then his eyes made out bulk in the shadow against the hut wall which after twenty seconds of concentration resolved into the shape of Garlan. The unusual shape of her tied-up skirt made the first recognition uncertain.

The shadow moved, straightened, a brief flash of paler color as her face turned toward Clay and he knew that she was aware of his presence. Then she was crouching again, moving toward the door, the knife a black shape in her hand as she moved out of the shadow.

Was she fool enough to try slipping into the hut? Martin would be sure to see her outlined against the entrance. It was foolhardy, and he could think of only one way to stop her.

He touched the implant and pressed with two fingers, activating his own broadcast range. "Martin!"

He spoke loud enough for Garlan to hear his voice; she stopped, looking toward him, angry. In his ear Clay heard another sharp intake of breath, the other agent unaware that his own words could be heard. Martin was listening.

"I know where you are," said Clay. "You can't get away. I know why you are doing this, Martin, but it isn't going to work. You've failed."

Still no answer; Clay could hear the blood pounding in Martin's skull as the other man stopped breathing.

"I don't want to kill you! Come out now!"

Garlan was moving back into the deeper shadows, Clay distracted from the hut entrance for an instant as he tried to follow her movement. He quickly returned his attention to the door, alert for anything the other agent might decide to do.

"Martin." He tried again. "Come out now!"

A spark flared in the shadows and Clay quickly looked that way again. Garlan had a fire flint and was striking it again, holding it against the hanging thatch. There were several more sparks, and then one landed on a straw, found fuel to feed its growth. Several seconds passed without apparent change, and then suddenly there was a worm of red coal several centimeters long. It flamed, and the fire licked hungrily at the material of the roof. Seconds later it flared again, and then was racing, a ravenous beast, through the straw thatching.

Clay heard Martin breathe sharply again, but for a minute he did nothing. Then the agent choked and coughed as smoke started to fill the interior of the hut. The stuff trickled into his lungs, sending him into a wracking spasm, and now Clay could hear him crashing about without the aid of the communicator.

"Martin!" he said, sharply. "You fool! Get out now while there's still time. Move!"

For another twenty seconds there was no response as the flames spread rapidly over the cone of the roof. More than half of it was burning now, the first section suddenly caving in and sending a shower of sparks into the sky. Clay watched in horror, not knowing what to do, as he saw Garlan move around the wall of the hut again, her knife once more ready.

There was another deep coughing, audible clearly in both the communicator and from the hut; and then Martin started toward the door, bending low at the waist to crash through the entrance . . .

Where Garlan was waiting, her knife slashing in a long upward stroke as the Earthman's arms flailed wildly. His impetus was enough to carry him half a dozen steps from the burning hut, and then he stumbled to his knee, his hand grasping the hilt of the blade that still quivered in his belly. Even as Clay rushed to him he fell forward, dead.

TWELVE

The pain burned deep through David Holland's neural system, permanently etched as a reminder of horror before the wrist device was finally released. He trembled violently as his body was returned to the control of his own conscious mind, his head jerking erratically. There had been the impression of elevators, corridors, cars, a long trip someplace in an enclosed vehicle, never once a release from the control mechanism.

They were in a large room with a long counter, manned by two blues at the moment; a bored technician sat in a chair that was tilted back against the wall, a portable tape reader competing with the blaring public channel on a wall screen. He looked up briefly as Holland was brought in, but the distraction was not important enough to cause him to stop the tape.

The first violent reaction to release was easing now, but the tremor held steady, Holland's hands shaking as he held them out before him. He was aware now of bladder pressure, painfully stabbing, and tried to speak. But his voice was only a croak, his tongue swollen in dry mouth. He touched it against his lips, mouth opening to relieve the pressure, and found that they were cracking. How long had he been under control? From the condition of his body, he knew that it had been hours.

"Come on, happy! Get movin!" One of the two blue guards who had brought him grabbed his elbow, forcing him to face the counter. "New fish for ya, locker. Big 'un."

One of the two men behind the counter came over, catching the small folio of documents as it was tossed. He broke the pressure seal, dumping the records and tapes out in a haphazard pile that he stirred with his fingers. David recognized his personal records in the lot, the ID card that had been a part of him since his elevation to yellow. The man spotted it, picked it up, holding it between two fingers so his fellow could see.

"Chee! A yellow." He grinned, showing discolored teeth that made Holland glance away. "We dun't see lotta these down here, do we, Harky? Knock 'em alla way down, smartass yellow!"

The technician heard the exchange, looked up to stare at Holland for a few seconds. Then the legs of his chair thumped on the floor and he was coming over to take the card from the blue's fingers. He studied Holland as he slipped the card into the reader on the counter, then let his eyes flick quickly over the transcribed information. His expression never changed as he finished, giving the card back to the blue and returning to his chair. The chair back thunked against the wall again, a line of white chewed through the painted plaster where it struck, and the tape reader went back into service.

"He ain't yellow no more," said the guard. "C'mon, blue, make 'em happy so's we c'n get."

The ID card was fed into a small machine attached to the side of the reader, and a moment later a duplicate popped out —a duplicate with several differences. The new card was featureless gray with a cord perhaps fifteen centimeters long attached to one corner. The yellow original was fed into the maw of another slot, and there was a grinding noise.

"Always wanted to powder a yellow," said the locker, grinning again. "Okay, happy, shuck 'em."

Holland stared blankly, and the man grew irritated. "Wotcher, empty in the ears, happy? Bare ass it, now!"

The guard chuckled. "Mebbe he thinks you're gonna bedboy 'em for a nickel, locker."

"Nah!" The man hacked and started to spit, then cast a quick look at the technician. He saw that he was being watched with a disapproving eye, so swallowed his phlegm, shaking his head. "He's too old. Bedboys gotta be pretty as slickies."

Holland understood the order at last and began unsealing his clothing. He found no particular embarrassment in nudity, but the circumstances were so degrading that his ears flamed. He worked slowly, his fingers fumbling with the seam locks, but at last everything was in a small pile. It was not much, as the remains of what had once been a proud citizen of Earth's highest classification.

At a gesture from the locker, David placed his garments on the counter. The man placed the gray card in the reader and keyed instructions, and in another half minute parcels began popping up from the counter: a one-piece coverall, underwear, socks, heavy shoes that looked uncomfortable. He went along the counter, assembling the items into a single pile which he slapped down before Holland.

"Gimme your wrist, happy. Not *that* one, your left one, empty! Doncher know your left from your right?"

Holland held out the demanded hand and the cord of the gray card was snapped in place, the end sealing itself seamlessly against the body. The locker tested it a time or two, David wincing as his hand was held tight and the cord cut into the flesh, a white line appearing.

"Lose it an' y' lose a week's joy juice," said the locker. "Get dressed, empty!"

Holland reached for the pile of new clothing as quickly as his general weakness and the bladder pain would permit. The clothing was correct in size, but the cut was unfamiliar and felt strange as it slid over his skin. The shoes were heavy and awkward on his feet.

"Harky, this'un's ready. Take 'em down to 34M."

Harky opened a flap in the counter and came out; he had been observing in silence through the ceremonies. Now he spoke his first word.

"Move." It came out painfully, his brow knotting. Holland waited for amplification, but nothing more came; at last he started toward the door through which he had apparently entered. It was the correct choice, Harky coming after him. The man was a plodder, moving slowly, but Holland was too weak to move any faster himself.

He waited in the corridor until Harky led him down a ramp three levels deep and out into another corridor. There were double doors spaced at long intervals, all of them closed. Harky led the way past several, and then turned, although there were no markings to identify his choice.

The door slid open to the guard and the bedlam of a public channel at peak volume exploded from within. Holland staggered under the noise level, his head immediately throbbing; he stumbled through and into a large room that seemed filled with hundreds of men, all dressed in clothing like his own. Most of them were slumped in rows of plastic chairs that were fixed to the floor, but a few circled the walls in constant motion while others sat on the floor itself. Most of the latter seemed to be ignoring the outsized screen that took most of the wall space at the front of the room.

Once in the midst of the maelstrom, the sound level was no longer quite so unbearable. Harky ignored it completely as he moved toward a small plastic desk in one corner that was manned by another blue. The man looked up as they approached, his attention torn from the screen.

"New fish or changer?" asked the blue, standing. Harky's brow furrowed in concentration, and the man waved the question off. "Forget it. Gimme your card, happy. Where you from?"

"I, uh, am new," said David. "Please! I have to use the toilet!"

"Gimme your card first. Yeah, do what you're told, happy, an' you'll be happy."

The card went into the reader, recording the safe arrival of the new man, the blue frowning as a slip of plastic popped out. He stared in intense concentration, his mouth shaping the symbols on the card.

"Okay, happy. We'll fin' your bed now an' you'll be all set. C'mon."

"I can't!" begged David. "Please!"

The blue was at first irritated, and then amused. "Okay, happy. Don't pee your pants—do it in there."

He laughed loudly as he pointed toward an open door, the joke going past the limited intelligence of Harky. Holland had no chance to share the emotion; he shambled toward the relief he needed, nearly doubled over now in his agony. When he made it through the door he was disturbed to find no private stalls, but any embarrassment was lost in his need.

He was still in pain when he finished adjusting his clothing and washed, but the intensity was no longer agonizing. He found drinking water at the end of the row of sinks and greedily took it in too fast, was sick almost instantly. When he again managed to wipe his mouth he took just enough of the water to ease the dryness, letting it soak in.

The blue had returned to watching the screen when David at last came out; he looked up, perplexed, as Holland shuffled to a halt before the desk.

"Wotcher want, happy—oh! You're the new fish. Wotcher want?"

"My bed," David said, patiently. "You said you'd show it to me."

"I did! Wotcher, empty in the ears? Wanna lose your joy juice, stupid?"

"Please." He pointed to the slip of plastic still on the desk. "I can read. I'll find it myself."

The blue stared in sullen anger, but after a moment he pushed the slip across to David. "Awright! Don' bother me no more today! Empty in the ears . . ."

He continued to mutter to himself as David took the slip and turned away, but his attention soon returned to the entertainment. Holland looked around the large room; at the back were long rows of tables with fixed backless stools. Two other large doorways opened off the main space, one to the right and one beyond the dining area. He chose the nearest one, which turned out to be the dormitory.

He stood in the doorway, staring; there were four rows of

bunks, tiered three high, the rows stretching away end to end for fifty meters or more.

The card in his fingers said B-24-2; the end of each row was marked with a large letter, and there were numbers on the side bar of each bed. Holland counted off until he reached 24, which was one from the far end; 2 was the middle tier, chest high. He leaned against it, eyes closing as the trembling suddenly became stronger. For a moment he continued to shake as his forehead rested against the mattress. Visions of the rows of bunks danced across his closed eyes in unending numbers: four rows, twenty-five beds to each, three tiers high. Three hundred beds in this dormitory, three hundred drones to share quarters with, when he had never in his life shared space with more than his parents, later Janice and his son. With Janice only for fifteen years now.

"You can't go to bed now, happy."

He looked up; an old man was standing there, a bent figure shaken by a palsy stronger than Holland's own. His hands were held before him, the tips of the fingers barely touching as they shook against each other, and now he shuffled a step closer.

"Blue catches you, he'll kick ass an' take away your juice tonight."

"I'm sick," David explained.

"Makes no diff'rence." He shook his head. "Go out in the court an' lay down there. Medic check before breakfas' only, 'less you're screamin'. You'll scream more if it ain't serious."

The old man peered from rheumy eyes that were clouded. "You ain't a changer. You been Declassified?"

Holland nodded. "Yes."

"Thought so. C'n always tell. These happies are empty in the ears, all of 'em. I was green. Green all the way. Had wife, gonna have kid . . . both gone." A tear was forming in the corner of his eye. "All gone. No more green no more. They put me here put me here."

David was embarrassed by the sudden deterioration in the old man as he turned away, shuffling off, muttering to himself as his head bobbed back and forth.

"What's your name?"

The other stopped, turned, blinked in surprise. "Name? Happy they call me, blue an' blue." He held up his dangling gray card. "No name no more, jus' this an' happy. Bruno it was, but no more. No more no green."

He turned again and was gone, leaving Holland to find the strength to move away from the bunk. He wanted only to sleep, to rest, to put his head down someplace . . . but he also knew better than to cause trouble his first hour in the barracks.

At last he retraced his steps to the door to the dayroom, looking out at his barracks mates; perhaps two-thirds of the chairs were full, and the sight of the nearest empty one tempting. But the blare of the screen was too much to contend against. The old man had said to go into the court; he looked toward the only other door, and saw that there was another large room beyond.

He started moving slowly in that direction, forced to stop and lean against the dining tables when he reached them. There was further pressure from his bladder as his body adjusted to the recent evacuation, the organ shaping itself again to a normal level; but he could not fight the journey to the facility again. The row of stools was tempting also, but they were circular and spaced far enough apart that he knew there would be no rest for his aching back if he did lay across them.

Then he was standing in the entrance to the court without remembering the last dozen steps. The court was a room as large as the other two, but totally devoid of furnishings or contents, other than the fifty or sixty men standing, walking, and lying about. The light source came from the ceiling, not bright enough to be distracting.

He moved in, wondering how those bodies lying in the center of the space could stand the obviously hard material of the floor. The chairs before the screen would be better. Then he saw that the composition of the floor changed three meters from the wall, and when he tested the new area, it yielded beneath his weight.

Holland sank to his knees, pain darting through them; then

put his hands out to cushion the blow as his body fell under. the no longer bearable strain of its own weight. He rolled, landing on his side with his knees drawn up; then rolled again, onto his back, the floor actually comfortable even though there was no pillow.

He shifted again, stretching out flat as his eyes closed in complete exhaustion and sleep finally . . .

Holland blinked, staring up at the ceiling, for a few seconds not remembering where he was. He started to glance at his wrist, but in place of his watch was only the gray ID card, dangling from its cord. The sight brought back awareness.

The other men in the room were moving toward the entrance in answer to the summons that had brought him from sleep. He tried to sit up, struggling to get his hands behind him for support, making it with an effort. His body seemed sore in every muscle, bone, and nerve-ending, but at the same time the terrible fatigue was diminished.

"Supper, happy." Old Bruno was standing just inside the entrance. "You don't eat it now, some other empty'll grab it. Long time till breakfas'."

Bruno turned after delivering his message and was gone before Holland could come to his feet. His balance was unsteady for the first few steps, and then he was able to move faster. He saw the others lining up before a row of robot vendors he had not noticed before; others were moving toward the toilet, so obviously there was time enough to relieve the pressure before joining the lines.

As he came back to the lines, his hands and face at least feeling clean, he saw the first men presenting their cards to a panel atop the vendors. Each was served with a tray, which was taken to the nearest table. By the time Holland received his own he had to weave through the rows of tables to find a vacant stool. He wanted to sit near Bruno, to pump the old man, but that table was filled. At last he settled for a spot between two greedy eaters who shoveled the food into their mouths as fast as possible.

He stared at his tray before picking up his implement; the menu was basic ration, nourishing though not particularly interesting. He began to eat as the man on his left picked up his tray to lick away the last traces of the food. Then the space was empty, giving him more elbow room and less disgust to work on his own meal.

The food did make him feel better physically. He had never imagined the conditions in a barracks, never even wondered at the life led by the drones. They were there at the bottom of the scale, the consumers who were fed and housed and entertained, but until this moment David Holland had no concept of what those three words could cover at the far end of the scale.

He finished, returning his tray to the vendor. There was a different blue on the desk now, Holland assuming that the shift changed every six hours. He started to return to the court, to escape some of the bedlam, when Bruno appeared before him.

"Juice time pretty soon." Apparently the old man had adopted him, a relationship David didn't mind. Bruno had information that he needed, could get no place else.

"I don't want any joy juice," he said. The old man immediately became cunning, casting conspiratorial glances to either side.

"Gi' it to me! I wan' it!"

"Fair enough—but I want some information. You help me and I'll give you my juice."

Bruno's head bobbed eagerly. "'s fair deal yes. Rots your brain terrible stuff yes. I was green. What you wanna know?"

David closed his eyes, thinking. "Do they ever let us out of here? Sweep the barracks?"

"Naw, not these empties. Dumbheads dumb. Sweep the busters, they got smarts."

"What are the busters?"

He shook his head. "Bad trouble yes. No good no good no good. No go there bust ass. Nonono!"

"All right." Holland held up his hands. "There must be some times when we get to go out. Think!"

"Nono." He shook his head again. "No never. No go out everythin' here. No."

"What about the women? There are only men here—when do they let us see the females?"

Bruno giggled; his tremor increased with his excitement. "No women, not empties like these. I was green; had wife, had kid. *They're* too dumb. Use bedboys, them that's smart enough to know what to do with 'em!"

"There must be *some*thing—sick call! You said medic check was before breakfast. They can't keep the sick here; where do they take them?"

"Shot in ass, kick in head. Go out dead, come back stupid. Nono. I was green now I'm stupid. Rotten juice rotten brain. Nonono." His eyes were tearing again.

"The hospital!" David insisted. "Where is it? Tell me, Bruno."

The old man was lost in feeling sorry for himself. He shuffled away, everything but his own loss forgotten. David stared after him in frustration, wanting to ask a dozen more questions. It was obvious that Bruno would have to be peeled slowly, the information extracted in small bits and pieces.

Escape. The thought had been there at the back of his mind even before his arrest, the eventuality considered and carefully walled away from his conscious mental activity. But he was here now, and knew already that it would be only a matter of time before he was as insane as Bruno if he was forced to stay in the barracks.

A sudden scream came from the screen; good ol' Doc Arko was at it again, he of the never-mentioned circus. Holland glanced that way just long enough to see a slice of quivering female mammary transferred to an instant range; seconds later Arko was indulging himself in his favorite food while his latest victim still pleaded for mercy.

Repulsed, Holland looked away again; he had never heard of the ancient pornographic meaning of the word circus, would not have understood the attraction of those who could be entranced by such sexual spectacle. Holland was a man of his own time, a well-adjusted individual who concentrated almost completely on his life's work. He knew affection for Janice, perhaps even love since they had married; the same emotion went to their adopted android son. But his strong feelings had been reserved for the Project, for the work being done to rescue the human race from complete degeneration to the level of the men around him.

These were tomorrow, and the thought was frightening.

"Juice time!"

The blue bellowed the words, bringing instant reaction; it seemed as though every man in the barracks was on his feet and lining up. David remembered his promise to Bruno; he joined one of the lines as the attendant gave the signal for the first men to present their cards. The plastic bottles popped out and were carried away quickly, some hugging the precious cargo close, others ripping away the tops and letting the effervescent narcotic gush into their greedy mouths. The line moved quickly.

Suddenly the blue stopped one man as he was about to grab his bottle.

"Not you, empty! You was stupid las' night. I tol' you not to be stupid las' night. No juice for you."

He grabbed the bottle away as the man stared, perplexed. At last he shook his head and moved away, the blue shoving the confiscated prize into his own shirt.

A minute later he did it again, Holland noting that he picked on only the least intelligent; presumably he also knew that they would not protest or fight back. By the time David had the promised bottle for Bruno the blue had half a dozen of the confiscated treasures, going back to the desk to stow them in the drawer. He kept one out, pulling the top and taking a deep suck, then wiping his mouth with obvious pleasure.

Many of the men were moving toward the dormitory, climbing into their beds to slip eagerly into the narcotic dreams induced by the juice. The ones David could see were not bothering to undress, even their shoes. The restrictions were obviously off now, and the idea of bed was the most tempting

thought of the day; but first he looked around for Bruno to
deliver the bribe.

Just as he saw the old man and moved toward him to press
his bottle into his hands, the door to the corridor opened, ad-
mitting a pair of blues. They stopped to glance around the barracks, idly curious; then moved to the desk to give the attendant a slip. He studied it, then stood up.

"Hollan'! Where you at, you dumb empty?"

David ignored the implied insult, moving as quickly as he
could toward the summons. "I'm Holland."

"Yeah? Gimme y'r card."

It was pressed into the reader, Holland standing patiently as
the blue attendant puzzled out the comparison of names on
the slip and the ID card. At last he released David's arm.

"Yeah, you Hollan'. You real smartass, huh? You in trouble
now."

His heart sank as the blue leered in triumph, wondering
what further undisclosed regulation he had trespassed. The
blues made no attempt to explain the rules to the newcomers,
assuming that they were drones from a lifetime of experience
and should know what not to do. The brief thought of planning escape disappeared again.

"Okay, Holland." One of the newcomers took his elbow.
"You belong to us now. Let's go."

He stumbled as he tried to keep up with them, expecting a
curse; but the blues immediately slowed their own pace to
match. Then they were through the doors and into the corridor, and the bedlam of the screen was cut off. There was a roar-
ing in his ears as his aural sense adjusted to the absence of dam-
aging sound, and then a high whining that seemed to go on
and on. He shook his head, swallowing, but the whine was
there, making their footsteps in the corridor sound strangely
distant.

They rose a level. This corridor was much the same as the
one just left, with a rank of doors exactly like the others. Assuming that they were more of the dormitories, he was not surprised when his escorts stopped before doors no more visibly

marked than any of the others. His brow furrowed as he tightened against the expected resurge of the sound storm as one of the blues pressed his palm against the key; he winced as the door slid back . . .

It was another complex like the last, but there was no rush of sound to overwhelm his senses again; the public channel was playing, but the sound level was turned down to a bearable and even reasonable level. As he followed the blues into the dayroom, he saw much the same arrangement already familiar, but there were immediate differences. The gray-uniformed men here were of an obviously higher level of intelligence; there were neither macro- nor microcephalics, no thickened brow formations, eyes dulled from inability to understand the complex world around them, no brains rotted from the narcotic that made barracks life bearable.

"All right, Holland. We have to check you in."

David looked at the man, saw that he was smiling. Yet it was not the sadistic grin of the warders he had seen to this point, no hint in the clear blue of the pupils that the mind looking out was planning to swing out in cruelty, catching an unsuspecting defective with sudden pain. Except for the cut of their uniforms, which marked their rank, these two men could have been citizens of any rank.

He followed the blue to the corner desk, presenting the card on his wrist to the man on duty. The attendant nodded a greeting, taking David's hand and guiding the card to the reader, rather than grabbing it and tugging, forcing the cord to cut into the flesh.

Puzzled, he turned to survey the large room. Now he saw that there were men in the chairs with joy juice cradled close, many of them obviously under the effects of the narcotic. But even those with lost eyes and vacant smiles were clearly not the low-grade defectives inhabiting the other ward.

There were a number of groups clustered around the dining tables. There were several card games going, and more than one chessboard in use; others were only talking, quietly and intently. One of them seemed familiar . . .

"Nathan!"

The technician heard his name called, rising and turning as Holland moved toward him eagerly, arms out to greet him. He came forward, a caricature of himself in the awkward-fitting drone coverall. His bony wrists protruded from the sleeves . . . and as they clasped arms, Holland saw that despite his clothes, he did not wear the dangling gray mark of the drone.

THIRTEEN

Garlan moved quickly, reaching the fallen Martin seconds before Clay. She rolled the body onto its side, the knees drawing up in a horrible cartoon of the fetal position. The hands gripped the belly, the edge of the blade slashing bone-deep in a final convulsive effort to avoid death, the fingers of one hand nearly sliced off.

Before Clay could give voice to his horror the little Karyllian was withdrawing the blade, wiping it on the bleached fabric of the priest robes. In the moonlight the stains on the cloth were black.

"Come now, Clahyh!" She rose to her feet, looking toward the center of the village for an instant, then back at Holland. "We must leave."

"And leave him?"

Surprise showed on her face. "And why not? Would you carry the meat with you? Let the carrion sweeps take him, he'll feel no pain for it."

"Why did you kill him?" he demanded.

Amusement briefly curled her lips. "You would rather be dead in his place? You said yourself not ten minutes ago that he was trying to kill us. Come! There's no more time to prattle. You may have no great liking for your skin, Clahyh, but I am most fond of my own."

Even as she spoke, the last words coming over her shoulder, she was leaving, her feet gliding softly across the packed ground. Clay could not make out the tiny noise of her footsteps —but the dead man's skull picked up the vibration of the movements, sending it through the still-activated communicator. It seemed to explode into his ear, a horrifying *sush-swish* that was a mockery of death's leaving. He stepped back, the thicker thudding of his heels also clearly audible. It was too much; he turned and fled, following the lead of the little woman.

They met no human obstacle as they continued through the darkness, the fire as yet not seen by those around the arena. Garlan reached the hakyar first and clapped her hands sharply in signal for them to kneel. Clay glanced up the knoll as he settled into the saddle, fastening his belt tightly; the huts were a cluster of dark shapes around the growing fire. He could not understand the failure of the villagers to see and give the alarm as sparks flew high into the sky, almost black themselves as they passed against the orb of the bright moon. They were falling back now, a gentle shower of pretty flakes that carried death as they settled onto other roofs.

There was a scream then in the night, and then a flare as another thatching caught suddenly; an instant later a third was blossoming the orange death-bloom, and the fire-beast was free to rage across the village in its entirety as an evening breeze suddenly gusted strong.

There were other screams now, and an uproar of shouting as Garlan urged her beast forward. Clay's mount followed automatically, the hakyar shifting gear under the woman's kicks to lurch into a semblance of a run.

"Garlan!"

The rush of their own wind tore the word away from his lips as Clay fought to maintain his balance, the belt about his waist not enough to hold him securely in place. The towering saddle lurched wildly from side to side with each long loping stride of the running beast. Clay was holding to the pommel with both hands, but there were times when a sudden jolt would throw him back, his head cracking painfully against the back rest.

Certain that the saddle lashes were about to tear free, Clay concentrated on falling, looking for the split-second warning that he was being tossed. The shock of Martin's death had been buried by the need to concentrate on this immediate moment, the questions that had started to rise in his mind shoved aside to fester by themselves. Since the first shout of the woman's name there had been no breath in his aching lungs to spare for words. The speculations were there, but would have to wait.

The village was well behind them now as the hakyar rushed over night-blind road. Clay prayed that the animals would not meet some obstacle in their path to cause them to stumble and fall, although the first mad rush had slowed somewhat. But there were no accidents; perhaps the beasts had night vision instantly adaptable to the changing luminance.

They flashed briefly into the open, a meadow silver-pale in the rising light of the bright moon; and then they were in woods once more as the road continued to rise toward the south. They were coming to the end of the valley, and the pace of the hakyar slowed under the strain of the hill. Then they were on the crest of the circling ridge and Garlan was at last signaling her beast to stop, reining back as her mount seemed to dance sideways a few steps until Clay came up to her.

She looked back. "They'll not come after us now."

She seemed satisfied as she watched the distant fire storm spreading through the huts of Turok's village. The circle was widening, a ring now, the center smoldering into darkness as the scant fuel of the huts construction material was quickly exhausted by the hungry flames. There were new flares of brightness coming from the very edge of the cluster, the village now a pyre that could be seen as dying even while the last new flares were touching off.

"What of the villagers?" asked Clay. "Did they manage to escape—the women, the children?"

She shrugged, unconcerned. "If they had their wits about them. Who is fool enough to stay in the midst of certain death?"

"They are of your blood!" Clay said, shocked again by her callousness.

"There are no strong blood ties among such, Clahyh. My fa-

ther sold me into slavery without protest from the others, as
was his right. Not one, not even Turok, cared what might be
my fate, so why should I now care for them?"

Clay was silent, having no answer. Yet he hoped that the villagers had managed to escape. He closed his eyes, trying not to
think. Garlan read his mood and let him be, and when he
looked again the ring of fire was noticeably lower, burning
down. He could bear to watch it no more.

He turned away, catching an expression of excitement on the
woman's face as she watched the final results of her work. He
was sure that it was lust, nothing more; her features clear in the
moonlight although it was not bright enough to bring color to
her skin. There was another fire in her eyes that seemed to
burn fiercely, if only the reflection of the distant flames.

He swallowed, uncomfortably aware of the tightness in his
chest, knowing that he was tensed by an emotion that he did
not clearly understand.

"Now!" The word exploded from his lips. "Tell me why this
was done, Garlan—tell me all!"

She smiled, again touched by a secret amusement; but there
was no irony in her expression despite her following words.

"You mean the men from heaven do not hold all of the secrets of the stars, Clahyh?"

She seemed much younger as their eyes met, locked; he wondered how old she could be. Sold into slavery and marriage at
eight . . . yet there was no indication that the body was anything more than a devilish child, black grime marking her face
again, her dress in tatters.

"You are Karyllian, Garlan? Nothing more?"

Her expression changed in an instant to anger. "Born on this
planet your Mah-tan called a stinking mudball!" she said,
fiercely.

"What do you know of other planets? Of Earth?"

"Only that there are worlds as great as Karyllia circling many
of the stars visible in the heavens—that Karyllia itself circles
the sun, rather than the other way about as is known in the
wisdom of the ages. You come from a world so far distant that

its sun is scarce a noticeable point in the night sky of Karyllia's bottom."

"And of Earthmen?"

Now wonder tinged her voice, as though she could not encompass the majesty of the universe but was now dealing with something close to her own understanding.

"You are men of magic, able to do marvels at a whim . . . and yet I have seen you close, Clahyh, and know that you are no more than men. You have enemies, even each other. You fight among your own tribes and villages."

"That isn't true," said Clay, quietly. "Earth is a planet of peace—there have been no wars among Earthmen for three centuries now. All are joined together in one great tribe, Garlan, one great city. None suffer from lack of anything needed to make life possible or comfortable."

"No enemies?" Garlan laughed in contempt. "Then why did Mah-tan hate you? You were his enemy, Clahyh, though you knew it not. He always intended that you be killed."

"He was greedy. Even in the best of worlds there are men hungry for power, for riches. But how do you know these things, Garlan?"

"He sent me to rob you in the city."

Another shocking statement; Clay frowned. "Of the filters?"

There was a blank look on her face, and then she remembered his earlier question.

"The talisman you showed me? I know it not, Clahyh. I was waiting for you when Mah-tan brought you down from the mountains, was with you in the caravan to Ahd-Abbor. You were never from my sight, even in your temple."

Clay had paid little attention to the dak herders and the other natives who traveled with the caravan; now he felt embarrassment at his lack of alertness. Perhaps there had been other clues he should have seen, telling him that Martin was an enemy before Peter Stone's revelations. As an observer for the trapped Stone, he was a poor choice, having failed miserably from the moment of his arrival on the planet's surface.

But . . . why? How could Martin have known that Clay was

here for a reason other than normal service, when he didn't know himself?

"Why rob me?" he demanded.

"To delay you. Mah-tan wanted you in the great square when the call came to evening services. I know not why, but he thought you would die then. He was angered greatly to discover that you still lived when he carried you into the temple."

The natives of the planet were not affected in the same way by the sonics of the Sanctum; for them the subaural sounds served only as a hypnotic compulsion. Martin must also have been responsible for the deactivation of Clay's shield . . . which meant that he had allies on the space station, for it could never have happened on the planet. He must also have stolen the filters.

Indeed, the man must have been angered to find that he was not delivering a corpse to the temple medics.

But . . . how time it so carefully? They could easily have arrived during the earlier hours of the day, which would have knocked that particular plan of assassination silly.

"How did he know that I would be in the square at the right moment?"

"He planned well, Clahyh. From the time you came down from the mountains he was seeking to delay the hour of your arrival. That was why you joined the caravan. He knew that the dak herders always came to the river in the late hours of the afternoon. Once across the river, he led you on a merry chase through the streets of Ahd-Abbor—a distance a man on foot should have covered in less than half the time he spent gulling you. He was leading you into trouble at every turn, Clahyh, and when he saw that time was still not dying fast enough, he signaled me to come against you for your purse."

Again Clay's ears flamed. But that explained how Martin knew that Garlan had been at work when the youth had not been aware of her touch.

"Why were you part of the affair—why now his enemy, Garlan? Something must have happened during the week that I was in the temple . . . what?"

The little woman was suddenly bitter, the lines of her face now harsh as her expression darkened. She sat straighter, the sudden movement causing the hakyar to shy away. Garlan patted the beast's neck while her eyes continued to burn against Clay's.

"He came to the thieves—not Mah-tan, but one of those with them. He told us of Earthmen, of other worlds, that the Temple of Light was a false religion churched only to swindle the true Karyllians out of their very world. He said he was friend, the others in their priest robes, enemy who would kill us all."

Her voice continued harsh with her hatred as the native woman told of the men who had pretended friendship to Karyllia, all the while planning the very course ascribed to the others.

"How did you learn that they lied?" asked Clay.

She slipped her hand into her pack, brought forth a small package, holding it up for Clay's inspection; he recognized a communicator powerful enough to reach the space station, and thus have its messages relayed to any point on the surface of the planet.

"I have heard Mah-tan speak to one of these boxes in the tongue of the Earthmen. They did not know that I understood their words, but they came among the thieves while I was being sold into slavery. When two of them talked together, they used always the same tongue; but they were always heard by the guild. In time we began to place meaning to their words, now we understand enough to know when the talk is of betrayal! *They* are the ones who would take Karyllia, kill us in our trust! They think us fools!"

"This happened since I came to Ahd-Abbor?"

"Not three days ago. I summoned a council of the guild, told them what I had heard. It is clear to us that Mah-tan and his kind are the enemy; therefore you must be friend, Clahyh. You *must* be friend . . . else we shall have to kill you all!"

There were still a dozen questions, more, tumbling to the center of his thoughts, each demanding attention, immediate explanation. He shook his head, then pressed the tips of his fingers against his temples to still the confusion. A few seconds later he looked at her again.

"You're a woman. Why did Martin choose you to work against me?"

"I'm a thief!" she said, proudly. "I am also inconspicuous; I can pass among a crowd as a boy, a man. Among thieves, it makes no difference what gender the gods gave you at birth. In the guild, only honor matters. And ability. I am a good thief."

"I'm sure you are," he said, dryly, knowing that her first discovery had been intentional. The second, earlier this afternoon, was only bad timing, the fortunes of chance. "Where did you get that?"

He indicated the communicator, surprised when she tossed it to him. He barely managed to catch it, juggling it for a second or two.

"I took it from Mah-tan's baggage this afternoon," said Garlan. This then had been the object of his search after the grenade attack—to summon help?

"Are only the thieves aware of the plot against Karyllia?" he asked.

"We need no others to help us crush an enemy, Clahyh. A thief is worth ten street dogs—a hundred of these village fools!"

She spat to one side, showing her contempt as she had this afternoon. Now Clay understood the reason for her earlier actions.

"Why were you on the road before us? Did you know that our path lay this way?"

"I followed you from Ahd-Abbor. The western road leads only through this valley, Clahyh, and when I became certain that that was your path, I cut across country to be ahead. Turok's is the first village on the road, so it was certain that you were heading there."

"The bandits? What charade were they?"

"None," she said. "They were genuine. I did not expect to live to see your arrival, once they began to circle in. But they

were playing with me, intending my death to be sweet enough
for a singer of lays."

Martin's response must have also been genuine, although his
motive could have been no more than boredom with the ride.
Certainly there was no reason for him to feel sympathy or affection for a victim of bandits . . . but his shock must have been
genuine to find that it was Garlan that he had rescued. There
had been no opportunity for him to speak to her once they
were in the village, so his curiosity must have been burning.
Until he saw the two of them leave the circle together.

Unless, of course, Garlan was now lying.

Clay studied her, closed his eyes to let the aura of her being
penetrate his consciousness. It was a trick that sometimes
worked when he was at Academy, when conditions were ideal.
Now there was no indication as to whether he was receiving
her emotional broadcast or not . . . but he had decided to trust
her.

She had been right about Martin's intentions.

"What now?" he asked. He turned to look back again, but
the burning village was visible as only a column of pale smoke
rising against the bright moon.

"We must return to Ahd-Abbor," said the woman. "But
we cannot go back the way we came. Mah-tan was to return
with your dead body, Clahyh, and the road will be watched."

Again questions! "But why?" he asked. "What good would
my death do him?"

"I do not understand the reasons. You were to be a symbol,
Clahyh, a signal for Mah-tan and his fellows to rise against the
people and destroy them."

The bloodbath forecast by Peter Stone. "How many of the
Earthmen are with Martin and the others?"

"I know some from seeing them together, but I do not know
them all. Others in the guild must know more, although many
by face, not name."

Clay juggled the communicator, debating. Call Stone and
warn him? The broadcast could be heard by others, who might

be—probably were—of the enemy. He rejected the thought, slipping the communicator within his robes.

"If we can't return by the main road, how are we to get back to Ahd-Abbor?"

"By way of Des-Abbor," she said. "The road splits, not too many granyar from here, and we will go to the seaport. There we can take a barge up the river, slip through the walls unseen."

"That will take days," he objected.

"Two days, no more, if we ride all night. Come! We have wasted enough time in chatter, Clahyh."

But even as she said it she was signaling her hakyar to kneel, untying the belt and slipping from the saddle. She tugged at the lace holding up her skirts, tossing it back to Clay; then shrugged the dress over her head.

Her naked body was gamin in the moonlight, looking like that of a young boy at one angle; then she turned slightly, and the shape of her small breasts was accented, lifting up strongly. Then she was pulling the robes she had worn earlier from her baggage, balling the dress and throwing it to the side of the road. She dressed quickly, then was back in the saddle and kneeing the beast into rising again.

Her heels dug into the animal's side, and once again they were moving.

Dawn found them well on the road to Des-Abbor, the land about them marshy now, the crop in the fields lining the road a water grain. They had been riding for hours when Garlan suddenly swung into a small settlement, a dozen houses set to one side of the now-broad road. There was other traffic, of the same sort that had been heading toward Ahd-Abbor from its surrounding district.

Clay took a deep drink from his canteen while Garlan argued with a boy tending a dozen shoat. He looked up, measuring the agent's form, and shook his head strongly. A coin was produced, bringing interest; a second ceased the argument. With the third he went into the largest house, coming out with a

woman who repeated his negative examination of the Earthman. The same three coins were enough to send her back inside, appearing several minutes later with an armload of
clothing.

"Change," said Garlan, signaling Clay's beast to kneel.
"Those robes mark you a tool of the priests, Clahyh. You cannot wear them into Des-Abbor."

He was glad of the chance to get out of the saddle, but he
took the new garments with an expression of distrust. They had
obviously known many wearings, and he wondered how many
natives of Karyllia they harbored now.

"Hurry!" the little woman said, impatiently. The farm wife
was standing by impassively, watching with something that certainly was not interest. "The tide will turn soon, and if we miss
it we will lose the day!"

Uncomfortable with the audience, Clay stripped off his robes
and donned the replacements. They were small, chafing in uncomfortable regions, and smelling of the former ownership. As
he discarded his own, the farm wife picked them up one by
one, and when the exchange was complete, disappeared with
them into the house.

They remounted, Clay's skin crawling with the anticipation
of being a Karyllian insect's meal; within minutes his expecta-
tion was rewarded. He slapped at his side as they continued on-
ward.

Des-Abbor was a city perhaps a tenth the size of the capital,
built on a broad delta. The river Greyat broke up into hundreds of little streams that meandered through the mud flats,
flooded when the rising tide sent salt water far upstream. As
they neared the city Clay saw that 90 per cent of its houses
were little more than huts, built on high stilts against the tidal
flooding. The buildings that were solid were on massive pilings
and deep stone foundations.

The main road they were traveling was built up now, pitch-
coated pilings driven deep into the mud, the roadbed nearly
ten meters above the flats. There were only a few branching
streets, narrower, most of the farmer traffic turning off onto a

broad stone-walled plaza short of the city's center. It had obviously been built over a period of thousands of years, to serve as marketplace.

In the distance Clay could see the masts of sailing ships, but they did not approach the harbor. Garlan turned her hakyar into the marketplace, where she sold both of the beasts to a dealer. The man was prepared to argue strongly about the price until the little woman suddenly had the point of her soul-blade touching the hollow of his throat. The merchant gulped, eyes popping, and quickly paid out her first demand.

There were several larger tributaries pushing through the flats as Garlan and Clay splashed through the puddles toward a group of small barges. The water was visibly rising, the boatmen preparing to cast off for the free ride that would carry them two-thirds of the way to Ahd-Abbor.

"Wouldn't a sloop be wiser?" Clay asked as Garlan approached a barge that seemed less loaded with cargo than the others. She shook her head.

"They will be watched too closely by Mah-tan's friends. By now his death must be known—he was supposed to report to them with the magic-voice at certain hours. We will take a barge. There are too many of them to watch."

The boatman seemed eager for passengers to supplement his cargo, but pressed his haggling more firmly than the dealer in hakyar. Clay saw that Garlan was impatient; but there was time yet before the water would carry them from the mooring. She indulged the man, both keeping a close eye on the rising stream. The bargaining broke off, a figure agreed upon, at the exact moment when the level was high enough for the ropes to be cast free.

The rising sun was bright in a cloudless sky, glaring down as the incoming tide swirled through the flats, turning the area into first a lake and then an extension of the sea. An awning had been erected over the rear half of the boat; a young boy in the stern tended to the rudder. Clay and Garlan watched the other traffic moving into the mouth of the river for a time, then crawled beneath the shelter, finding scant space to sit among the cargo. They were crowded together by lack of room, Garlan's back pressing against Clay's; after a moment she lay down, Clay following suit, to seek the sleep that had been denied during the night ride.

The next time Clay's eyes opened it was night; the late tide was running with them. There were uncountable aches and pains in his body from the uncomfortable position and from the native inhabitants of his clothing, and at some point he had shifted to his back. Garlan was pressed against his side, curled like a child, innocence in her face when he glanced down that made it difficult to recall the glee with which she had sunk the knife into Martin's belly.

She sensed his alertness, opened her eyes to the compromising position. She smiled, but did not move, only her eyes going to the bow where the boy was heating a fish stew over a small brazier. Several minutes passed, during which Clay felt almost at peace; then the meal was shared out, and it was necessary to sit up to accept it.

They moved quietly through the night, the only occasional sound that of a night amphibian along the shore and the constant chorus of insects over the water. There were other barges on the water, but the rule of the river seemed to be silence during the hours of darkness. Clay dozed, then awoke to see the boy with his pole again. He shifted position slightly, Garlan's head hurting against his upper arm, cutting off the circulation. This time he stayed awake for a long time before sleep once more captured him.

Dawn found them beneath the walls of Ahd-Abbor, moving through thick traffic that was heading as much south as north. Garlan was sitting up beneath the shelter, alert to the other craft and then to the shore as they came into the area of wharves. The boatman moved toward a rickety wooden dock that extended its narrow runway well out into the river, finding a place near the end to tie up. Before the boat had stopped drifting the boy was scampering up the ladder.

The two passengers started out from beneath the shelter, when suddenly Garlan caught Clay's arm, holding him back.

"Look!" she commanded.

He followed her pointing finger to the quay, where a man in the white robes of the Eternal Light seemed to be casually watching the river traffic, from time to time moving a few paces farther along.

"I know him!" she said. "He is one of those with Mah-tan!"

FOURTEEN

"David!" Nathan was smiling, but even as he spoke Holland's name the look on his face turned to concern as he took in the sunken eyes, the tremor in his body. "Are you all right?"

"I don't know," he admitted. "Let me sit."

The technician guided him to the nearest stool, one of the men vacating it for him. Nathan was shocked by the appearance of Holland, who seemed to have aged half a lifetime since the moment of his arrest.

"What did they do to you, David?" he asked.

Holland held his hands apart, his head shaking; tears were forming in his eyes, and he felt shame. But the reaction was beyond his control. He blinked, and the first tears broke free to trail wetly down his cheeks.

"I don't know. Where are we . . . where is Janice?"

"In St. John, of course. Janice is safe. David, what have they done?"

A man across the table spoke: "Left him in restraint, I'd say. How long was the cuff on you, Dr. Holland?"

He lifted a hand, let it drop. "From the moment of the trial until they brought me here this afternoon. How long was that?"

"Twenty hours or more!" The man cursed. "And full power, from the looks of you. Somebody wants you dead!"

Holland's eyes closed as he gave in to the weakness that washed across his body. He began to sway, then hands were grabbing either arm, helping him up. They were carrying his weight now as he passed into unconsciousness.

He opened his eyes to find a stranger seated beside his bed, booktape in hand. The slight movement as Holland turned his head caught his attention, and he looked up.

"Good morning, Dr. Holland. How are you feeling?"

"Weak. Terribly weak."

"That's quite understandable. You're suffering from exhaustion, dehydration, and electrical shock. I really don't understand how you managed to make it up from the zoo on your own."

"Where is Nathan?" He saw that he was in a dormitory.

"He'll be back soon." The man bent, came up with a medical kit, putting it in position over Holland's bare chest. There was a cool tingle as the kit read his vital signs and injected medication.

"Thirsty," said Holland.

The man nodded as he removed the kit and sealed it, then reached below David's line of vision to come up with a sealed bottle from which a straw protruded. He held it to Holland's lips, letting him suck eagerly.

"Electrolytes, Doctor. Now try to get some more sleep."

He complied, eyes closing immediately to sink into a dreamless rest.

When he awoke again the chair was still in place, but empty; before he could move, Nathan and the medic came into the dormitory. They were smiling.

"Feeling better, David?" asked the technician.

He blinked, checking the responses of his body. "Yes—much better," he said, surprised.

"You can sit up now," said the medic. "In fact, please do, Doctor."

Their hands were there unnecessarily to help him. David shrugged them off, swinging his feet to the floor and bending forward to avoid cracking his head on the bunk above. He held out his hands, and saw that there was barely the faintest tremor. Then he stood.

"Sleep is always the best medication," said the medic, bending to pick up his kit. Now David realized that he was not dressed in the drone coverall.

"I'll check in this evening," the medic said, more to Nathan than to his patient. "I'm sure there'll be no problem."

Nathan nodded. "Thank you, Harron."

Holland waited until the man was gone, then turned anxiously to the technician. "Where is Janice?"

"Smuggled to safety, David. At least for the time being. We were preparing to do the same for you, but they moved too quickly after the trial. You were gone, and it was not until the next day when they delivered you here that we knew what had happened."

Holland remembered the interminable ride as a measure of the horror of the cuff. Was it all a sham? Perhaps they had actually sent him to another district, then returned him for some reason of their own.

"How did you find me?"

"The technician in receiving sent through the word as soon as he came off duty."

"I don't understand. This . . . any of this. This is a barracks, but these men are nothing like those where they first put me."

"Wiley's sadism, David. You were with defectives, the severely retarded. It could have been worse; there are barracks for those unable to care for themselves at all, the incontinent and the mindless."

"But the blue warders seemed no better than the others!"

"For the most part, they aren't; it's not a popular assignment. The blues are after all drawn from the general drone population, David. For the most part they are no better than the masses. The exceptions have been carefully selected."

He saw the lack of comprehension and sighed. "David, you were born too high and selected too high. Sit down; it's time you learned the truth of our marvelous twenty-fourth-century world."

Holland did as the younger man directed, listening intently, and then with astonishment as Nathan explained the facts of modern life.

"Over half Earth's population is in the barracks, David—a

total waste of not only what natural abilities might exist, but of
life itself. It's true that many of them are well below the norm
of intelligence, but except for the defectives, they are permitted
to breed freely. Yet how many citizens do you know who have
brought more than one child into the world—how many have
brought none?"

He thought of Janice, and felt a vague guilt. There was no
reason for them not to have a natural child, but the subject
had never come up. They had married to provide shelter for
Clay, their first successful android. Perhaps marriage would
have come anyway, considering the closeness of their association; but it had originally been a matter of convenience to their
work, nothing more.

"That is the reason for the regression in intelligence, David
—nothing more! Bad breeds bad, the defective genes multi-
plying and reinforcing each other, driving out the good. If only
the best were allowed to breed, you'd see an immediate reversal
of the trend."

"Population control was outlawed by the Compact," said
Holland, automatically. "Whether to have children or not is a
matter of personal conscience."

"Yes," said Nathan. "Outlawed because there was no need
for it when the Compact was drawn. There was no population
pressure to force an unpopular and distasteful weeding out of
the unfit. But that no longer holds true. Unless a program is
put into effect within this generation, the situation may be irre-
versible."

"The androids . . ."

"A race of their own, David, as different from the natural
race as the hominids of Karyllia and Locane! They are men,
but they do not share our ancestry—only the prejudices of our
history. There are four races of men now, perhaps more on
worlds yet to be discovered. They can co-operate—*must* co-
operate, for their mutual interests—yet they must also remain
separate and distinct, to develop their own potential without
help and without hindrance."

"You're saying the Guided Worlds policy is wrong?"

"It is." He began to pace now in his animation, six short steps and then a reverse turn. "Not for the reasons claimed by the Firsters, of course; but for the more fundamental reason of the right to freedom. We made a mistake fifty years ago when we began the policy."

"We?" Holland raised an eyebrow. "Are you speaking personally, Nathan?"

"Who do you think runs the world, David? Not the politicians; they only govern, fill the service slots that require bureaucratic inertia to function properly. No, Earth is run by the technicians—has been since the days of the twentieth century. Without us, the machinery would come to a stop; nothing would function."

"You support the technology, yes . . . but do you also claim actual power?"

"We created the Reformationists, David. And the Humanity Firsters."

The statement was the most shocking of all. Holland stared at him a moment, then shook his head.

"What do you mean? In what way did you 'create' them?"

"I don't speak of myself," said Nathan. "Of course not, David—I'm not paranoid. But the technicians have been banded together since the time of the Compact, puppet masters, if you wish. We pull the strings, people like Wiley respond. Few of us have high position, for we don't wish to become obvious in our control. The puppets might revolt."

"The Reformationists are founded in madness," said Holland, slowly. "Why are they necessary?"

"Because the Compact is strangling Earth! For three centuries the planet has been bound by the provisions of that long-ago agreement which was based upon the political necessities that came from the Bad Years. Earth has changed in those centuries, David. Our needs are different from those of the men who wrote the Compact and sealed it. Yet in those three centuries not one word of the original has been changed. New sections have been added to deal with new situations that did not then exist, but the social structure of the planet has been strait-jacketed for three hundred years."

"The Compact must be changed?"

"Not changed, David—scrapped! We must start fresh. But to do that, it is necessary to plant the seed of change early. That is why the android project was proposed to the President thirty years ago. Even then it was obviously a blind alley, but it was a small violation that could lead the way to greater changes.

"Wiley is our man completely," he said, sitting on the edge of the bed. Ten seconds later he was up again, and pacing. "Once the Reformationists take over the government he will introduce a resolution to study the genetic defects of the race. From that, it is just a step to the course that has been needed from the beginning."

Holland felt a sinking sensation in his gut. He reached out to grab Nathan's arm, forcing the younger man to stop, to meet his eyes.

"Did you reveal the Project to Wiley?"

"No, David. But if it had been necessary, I would have. The President saved me from the betrayal. He has been studying the secret diaries of his predecessors, one of whom was foolish enough to record the details of the Project. Perhaps each new President should have been informed, but it wasn't felt necessary. Shocked by the violation of the Compact, he called in Wiley."

It wasn't much, but it was a personal satisfaction. Still, it was tempered by the knowledge that thirty years of his life had been spent in a charade devised by others.

"What happens now . . . to me?"

"For the moment you are safe here, David. We use this ward as a cover—nearly a hundred of the men work for us, knowing that in time they'll be selected as blues. It isn't much, but it's better than a lifetime in the barracks."

He shook his head. "Waste! Over a billion human beings, useless no matter what their abilities. The planet is too small, David, and we can't send more than a fraction of them into space. The population must be cut in half, starting now. Perhaps even that will be too much; if so, then it will be cut again. It *will* be, David; it *must* be! If Earth collapses into barbarism, the planet cannot support another climb from the beginning. Only technology can support continued superior life."

"I want to see Janice," said Holland. "Can you make the arrangements?"

"Tomorrow. There will be a sweep for another Firster demonstration."

David nodded, satisfied. "What of my future? What plans do you have for me? I don't want to spend the rest of my years here."

"So long as the Reformationists hold the government you will have to remain hidden. Once the Compact is set aside, things may change, but for now it will be best to get you off the planet entirely."

Holland thought that his capacity for surprise had been filled to surfeit by Nathan's revelations, but this new idea made him blink.

"Leave Earth?"

"Karyllia would be best, but we don't know yet whether Stone has managed to put down the Reformationists." He seemed embarrassed. "In this instance we appear to have created a Frankenstein's monster, David. The psychometricians miscalculated the level of xenophobia present in the human mind. Originally it was a survival instinct, but the gene passing it has never been isolated."

"Clay is on Karyllia."

"I know, David." His voice softened. "I also know that he was the first successful android."

"Only Janice knew that. There are times when I forget myself. He is my son, Nathan, no matter what the means of his birth. *Our* son."

"You can't force his future, David. You can't make him something that he is not. He must be told, and he must choose for himself."

Nathan placed his hand on Holland's shoulder. "The secret

of Clay's birth was in the diaries released to Wiley, David. The Firsters know what he is. He will never be able to return to Earth, no matter what happens on Karyllia. It is best that you and Janice join him there."

"If he lives," Holland said, bitterly.

The next morning the word passed quickly through the barracks of the upcoming sweep. Holland was reminded of a childhood outing he'd once taken with a group of other children in his school class, the eagerness and anticipation as great. The emotion was one he shared now.

They were marched in a group to the drop shafts, for the first time an inkling of his location revealed. They had been high in the tower; it took a long time for the shaft to deliver them to ground level, where they were loaded in buses and lifted into the air. He craned to see out of the window, orienting himself to the city; the barracks were north of Government Center, site of the demonstration.

They were not the first to arrive; already there were more than a thousand drones assembled, receiving final instructions as team leaders passed among them, handing out pickets and individual noisemakers. He looked for Nathan, for Janice, for any familiar face; but there were only those who had come with him in the sweep.

At last they were ready, assembled into a form of order. The signal was given, and they marched toward the government buildings several blocks distant. The sign in David's hand was a flasher, its alternating red and green proclaiming "Earth for Earthmen!" over and over.

He felt hemmed in by the mass of humanity as they moved closer to their goal; even the barracks hadn't been this bad. Then they were there, a sound car moving slowly ahead of them—slowly enough that they managed to overtake it. In five minutes David was abreast of it, glancing idly at the sealed windows.

The door beside him irised opened, the interior darkened so that he could see only a vague shape in the far corner as he glanced in. He started to pass by, when suddenly the person spoke.

"David!"

He stopped, the shock of recognition catching him by surprise even though he had been anticipating her voice. A quick glance around showed that the team leader was concentrating on something ahead; he ducked through the door, which immediately closed again, the interior lights coming on.

"Janice!"

She smiled, holding out her hands. He moved forward, then realized that he was still holding the picket. It was impossible to ignore as both sides flashed the message, but he shoved it into the corner, then embraced his wife.

"Thirty years wasted!" he said, a moment later.

"Not wasted, David. It served a very important purpose. Even if it had not, the idea of research in itself has high value. The Project did solve the problem it was given."

"You knew from the beginning?"

"Yes. I was one of the committee that originally proposed the Project. We fed it to Charles, let him carry it to the President."

"Did he know the real purpose of the charade?"

"Yes, always. It was necessary to tell him everything to show him the necessity of our program."

"Then I was the only fool!"

He slumped back into the seat, staring at his hands as they fell between his knees. Janice reached to touch him, gently.

"You are not a fool, David. Never a fool. You were given the information necessary to develop a program that could lead to the ending of the Compact, and you served with the highest ability."

They were silent together for a moment, hands meeting, the contact between flesh and flesh reassuring to the man. But Holland could not forget that he had lived thirty years of blind service to a falsehood.

"Knowing the reason for the regression," he said, "why did you never have a child of our own, Janice?"

"I tried," she said, her voice so low that it was difficult to hear over the rush of sound surrounding the conditioned car. "For years I tried, David. I didn't want you to know of the failures. In time I stopped trying. Clay may be android, but he is our son. That will never change."

The car lurched to a stop, throwing them both forward. He helped her catch her balance, and then held her close again. When they at last parted he saw the tears in her eyes, touched them with his finger.

"They want us to leave Earth, Janice."

She smiled again, blinking. "Why stay? Our work here is done. If we can go to Karyllia, we'll have a whole new planet with nothing but projects that need directing, David. The future is there now, at least for us."

It was a comforting thought, spoiled only by his knowledge that, unlike themselves, Clay was in danger of his life . . .

If he still lived.

FIFTEEN

Clay studied the white-robed Terran a moment, recognizing his face. The man was unmistakably watching the water traffic, his eyes passing with apparent idleness over every boat that came near.

At that moment Garlan touched his arm, pointing farther along the quay to where another white robe was standing.

"How do we get by them?" he asked.

"Wait, Clahyh."

The boatman watched curiously as she slipped from beneath the awning, moving as agilely as the boy before her. The priest saw her head appear over the dock, watching without recognition as she finished the climb and sauntered slowly toward him. Then she was past, disappearing into a narrow alley.

As the minutes passed slowly Clay saw the boatman's boy returning with a factor in tow, the man obviously bored by the whole affair of trading. He came out to the end of the dock, standing there while the boy scrambled back down the ladder to begin a desultory conversation with the boatman. They began to argue back and forth, neither showing that his heart was in it, while the boy pulled samples out of the various piles.

Clay listened for a few minutes, but grew bored. He looked back at the wharf and saw a ragged urchin. The lad approached the Terran, tugging at his robe—and Clay recognized Garlan in another change of clothing, her pigtail now dangling sloppily over one ear.

The priest glanced down, annoyed, as Garlan's head bobbed animatedly. A question was asked, and she pointed toward the alley; even from the boat Clay saw the suspicion on the agent's face. He looked toward his fellow just within his sight while Garlan renewed her plea. At last he shrugged, and turned to follow her scampering lead.

They reached the alley, the agent stopping to bark another question at Garlan, who was already slipping into the narrow and dark way. She said something that angered the man; he started to reach for her, moving into the alley a pace or two . . . and from nowhere two men appeared behind him, their shoulders jerking with a sudden violent movement.

The Earthman started to turn, his head snapping back in shock . . . and then he was sagging, caught before he could collapse and dragged farther into the alley by the two assassins. A moment later Garlan reappeared, darting quick glances in each direction; satisfied that the deed had been unobserved by anyone on the quay, she came toward the dock, Clay already on the ladder.

He stopped halfway up when the communicator spoke in his ear: "Barrett? Is that you, Barrett?"

Garlan had stopped when she saw him emerge. Now he came up to peer carefully over the top of the dock. The other agent was taking an uncertain step this way as he slipped over, shrugging and stooping to minimize his height.

"Barrett! Answer me, man! Where are you?"

Garlan had turned, was a dozen paces ahead of him when Clay reached the quay. He caught her at the mouth of a street, pausing there just long enough to glance at the Earthman, who was a few steps closer, looking about in confusion. He was paying them no particular attention, however, even when he made up his mind and began to walk that way.

He would find the dead man in another minute; would he give the alarm over the communicator? There was no sign of the assassins.

"Fellow thieves?" asked Clay.

"A summons from the soul-blade cannot be denied," she said.

They pushed through streets as narrow as the alley, the way as twisting and turning as when Martin had led him on a merry chase. Several times they saw white robes, some of whom Garlan recognized as Martin's fellows. When that happened they ducked back, taking another way. Clay kept his attention on the communicator, but there was no outcry from the dock area.

"I must reach the leader of all priests," he said once when they had ducked through a bazaar, stopping for a moment in a shaded garden court that seemed peaceful and still. Then the owner's servant appeared at the door, shrilling at them to be away.

"Mah-tan's fellows are everywhere," she said. "You cannot dare the temple."

"I must see him!" he insisted.

Doubtful, she asked for a description. "I know him, Clahyh. I will bring him to you."

It was said with such assurance that he did not doubt her. But obviously she had changed her mind about the course they were following; now they cut through side streets, coming at last to a seedy tavern in a district best described as disreputable.

There were a score of idlers lounging about the tables as they entered, all of them ugly, none of them in pleasant mood. They stared at the newcomers as Garlan moved to the kitchen to speak to the innkeeper. Then she gestured, and Clay followed her through the tavern to the back of the building where rickety outside steps led to the upper stories. She started up, the wood creaking and shaking alarmingly when Clay put his weight on the first step. But it held, and he followed her.

The second story was obviously of a different construction than the first, and the third and fourth of other periods yet. There was no landing, just a door opening off the stairs which she opened without waiting for an invitation. Clay slipped in behind her.

The room was windowless, lit only by a few smoking oil lamps. Clay blinked at the change, making out a few more of the tavern tables and vague shapes around them. Then as his eyes adjusted, he made out their features.

He started to speak, but Garlan turned swiftly, her hand going across his face.

"Here you will be silent, Clahyh, until invited to speak!"

"A stranger?" asked a voice from the darkest corner. Then he cursed: "He is one of them!"

He came to his feet, burly for a Karyllian and broader through the shoulder than Clay. But he was half a head shorter, his legs bowed widely as he moved, his hand bringing out his knife.

"No!" cried Garlan. "This is the one they hate—the one they call android."

For a moment the word passed Clay's notice, distracted by the other problems. Then his ears pricked, his mind sorting her words again to pick it out. Android? What did they mean? Androids were forbidden under the Compact.

Tension held for a moment, and then the burly one sheathed his weapon. "You should not have brought him here, Garlan. It is too dangerous."

"He can help," she said, strongly. "Not all of the white robes are enemy, Burrus."

"Then why do they hide in their false robes behind their false gods? What do they want?"

Clay watched Garlan look at him, the deep wells of her eyes catching the flickering lamplight and sending it back. At the moment she seemed very much a woman, despite her clothes and despite her surroundings. He wondered which element was strongest now . . . woman, or thief?

"Can you answer?" she asked.

He chose his words carefully, trying to find phrases that would not antagonize the short-tempered audience. There was doubt in their attitude, the natives unable to understand the idea of philanthropy for unselfish reasons. It was alien to their very being, and at last the burly man shrugged.

"You speak of fools, android. We thieves have fattened on fools since the first purse was worn."

"Martin and the others enlisted your help for the promise of treasure . . . a treasure you would never enjoy. I offer you life!"

"Which we have now."

"And which you can lose in darkness, never knowing death is

near until your lungs choke, your food no longer nourishes you, the water you drink poisons you!"

"We *must* help them!" said Garlan. "I do not wish to die without honor, Burrus!"

The other argued for another ten minutes, but at last he was beaten down. He retired to his corner, dismissing her from his presence.

"Do as you must, Garlan. Any foolish enough may join you, but I think you're mad."

Satisfied, she began to strip out of her clothing, going naked to a large chest in the corner of the room. She ignored the male eyes watching her body as she grunted against the plank lid of the chest, finally raising it; then she dived into the haphazard bundles of clothing within, coming up with a dress that would let her pass muster as a temple servitor.

She smiled at Clay as she donned it, then combed out her hair. He saw her slip her knife into place beneath the clothing, and then an old woman's cowled cloak hid the dress from prying eyes. A moment later she was gone, leaving Clay in the company of the thieves.

Who ignored him.

Which left him nothing but his thoughts as occupation. After a time he activated the communicator, increasing the gain, but could pick up no hint of activity in the streets outside. Even when he brought out the instrument Garlan had confiscated from Martin, he could get nothing. The temple and the space station were silent.

Now the tag she had given him came back to taunt. Clay dredged his mind for the information it held about androids, but came up with virtually nothing beyond the historical fact that they had been outlawed by the Compact. There was something terrible in the connotation, but he knew no more.

He certainly wasn't android!

An hour dragged slowly, each minute ticked off on his mental clock; and then a second. The best part of the third was gone as well before a change occurred. During that time several of the men in the room had left, singly, while others had come in. All ignored him.

When the door opened again he glanced up, expecting no more than another of the thieves. There were other women in the room now; for a time they had been in the majority. Then he recognized Garlan and sat up straight as she brought in a street beggar whose robes were barely more than rags.

The beggar blinked against the dimness, but Clay had already recognized Stone. He jumped to his feet, moving to greet him.

"Clay! It is you—this woman said Martin is dead!"

He nodded, looked at Garlan. "What else did you tell him?"

"Only that you were here, Clahyh. And in danger."

"Then you'd better sit down, Peter."

Stone followed the suggestion, listening intently to everything Clay said. When the youth finished the man turned to Garlan.

"All thieves are in alliance with the Reformationists?" She stared blankly, and he added, "Martin and his fellows?"

Garlan looked to Burrus, who had gone out twice during her absence, each time returning after a few minutes. Now she was deferring to his position.

"We hold no alliances," he said gruffly.

"You aided them," pointed out Stone.

"We served for pay, no more. We owe them nothing."

"We owe them our soul-blades!" the little woman said, fiercely. "They lied to us, Burrus! Will you lie down in the street to be trampled by their hakyar?"

The thief-leader scowled, Clay wondering if she had punctured his pride too deeply. He slammed his fist against the table, ready to shout at her, when Stone put another question that distracted his anger.

"How many thieves are there in Ahd-Abbor?"

Burrus blinked, looked quickly at several of the other men. "As many as there are stars in the sky!"

"I doubt that," Stone said, calmly. The night sky of Karyllia was far richer than Earth's in stellar census. "Nor do I care what crimes your people may have committed against the citizens of this city. You have worked with the men who plot to destroy your race, Burrus—not just some, not even many, but all Karyllians will die if they have their way! Thieves among them!"

He bent suddenly, touching the heel of his boot, then straightened to toss something against the wall. Clay was on his feet in horror, crying out.

"No, don't!"

The grenade bounced off the wall, hitting on the floor, at last self-destructing. A little cloud of white vapor boiled up, acrid in smell, as Clay closed off his breath and rushed forward to sweep Garlan away. But the gas moved swiftly, the thieves coughing and hacking and pawing at their eyes.

Stone stood, back of his hand over his face, and moved to open the door. Tears stung Clay's eyes as he saw that the thieves still lived, the gas only one of the training samples. It lacked even the regurgitant.

"That is what will happen to you, Burrus, if the Reformationists are not stopped. Except they will not use something mild enough to bring only tears."

Clay thought the thieves were ready to tear Stone apart, but the other knew what he was doing. The example was graphic, penetrated instantly in a way that they could not argue away as they had with Clay's earlier words.

"If we help you, you will give us the poison clouds?" Burrus asked, warily.

"To use against your innocent fellows?" Stone shook his head. "No, Burrus. You've protection enough against any weapon Karyllia can produce. I will reward you, however—if life itself is not reward enough. What pay were you promised by the others?"

"The riches of the temple, after you were all dead."

It was Stone's turn to blink, but his face remained impassive. "Do you believe now that they intend to reward you in the way they promised?"

Again scowling, Burrus glanced at Garlan, then at several of the others, seeking support. The little woman was fiercely on the side of the Earthmen; the others showed their uncertainty by looking away.

"What will you give?"

"Riches enough to keep you in comfort the rest of your days. Treasure to make you a man among the greatest men of Ahd-Abbor. For your people, a thousand measures of silver."

"Each?" he insisted.

"Of course."

He nodded. "Very well, man of another world. Seal it in blood."

He drew his knife, drawing a line from his wrist to the elbow on the inside of the forearm. For an instant the line was white against his flesh; then the blood welled up dark and rich. He wiped his hand through it as Stone drew a knife of his own, repeating the operation, his face impassive. He followed the Karyllian in every way, reaching out to clasp hands with him. Burrus ground their palms together, mixing their blood, then held his hand up to show the red smear. Again Stone did the same.

"The others also swore in blood," said Burrus, softly.

"You know that they lied. What is the price of breaking the oath?"

"Death!" It was barely a whisper. "I care not for your riches, Earthman. A thief can steal the riches he needs. I have tested you only because this one insists that there are men of honor among you despite the evidence." He indicated Garlan with a twist of his head.

"If she is wrong—if you also lie—then all Earthmen will die. I swear it upon the life of every thief!"

Clay was conscious that he had been holding his breath. He let it out with a rush, clasping Stone's shoulder in relief.

"Good! We're in agreement with the guild, Peter—but what do we do? How will we take them without alerting the lot?"

"The guild will do it for us," said Stone.

It was night when they reached the central square, which

was lit now only by the torches in front of the Terran temple and the ancient citadel. The fire cauldrons burned balefully in the eyes of the Sanctum, but there was no illumination from that source.

Despite the darkness there was much traffic circulating through the square. Clay was reassured by the knowledge that much of it was there in support of him, but he felt foolhardy nevertheless as they moved toward the temple, Stone and Garlan with him.

The two Earthmen paused fifty meters short of the steps as they saw a white-robed priest come out of the temple, standing there a moment to stare toward the red eyes burning at the other end of the square. He paid no attention to the natives drifting by, knowing that mendicants were being bedded down for the night on the floor.

"Do you know him, Garlan?" asked Stone, softly.

She shrugged. "I think so." She moved toward the steps, hurrying up them to stand just below the priest, tugging at his robe. He glanced down, irritated.

"If your belly is empty, boy, the kitchen is still open."

"Mah-tan is dead!" she said.

"What?" He reached out to grab her shoulder. "Show me your badge!"

She slipped her knife out so that he could see the blade, and he nodded. "The other did it," she added. "The one they call android."

"Where is he now?" he demanded.

But Garlan had turned, was hurrying back the way she had come. The agent cursed, started to turn back into the temple, then changed his mind, following her. Clay held his breath, expecting to hear a warning cry over the communicator; but there was nothing, even when he reached the bottom step and moved out.

Suddenly there was a knife at the priest's ear, the point pushing through the tiny circle to shatter the communicator before it could be activated. Clay thought he heard the briefest part of an in-drawn breath, but it might only have been his own.

A dozen natives were around the agent now, bearing him down, other knives threatening any movement to protect himself. They were stripping his robes away, pulling his boots from his feet, a woman bundling them together and wrapping them in a cloth to cover the white. She hurried off, brushing past Clay and Stone as they converged on an alley toward which the naked agent was now being hurried. They met him there, carrying him into darkness . . . but not before he saw their faces.

"Now!" Stone touched Burrus' shoulder and the tip of the thief's blade sank a centimeter into the flesh of the agent's throat. "You'll talk, Worrel, or you'll never see the light of another morning."

The man choked. "You're insane! The Compact!"

"No, the insanity is elsewhere. And the Compact is dead, destroyed by your scheming. The Reformationists may have Earth, but they will not have Karyllia! I honored the Compact, but Martin is dead and there will be more if you fail to answer my questions. Burrus!"

Again the point of the blade pressed farther, causing blood to spurt; it trickled warmly down the agent's throat. He knew that he was as close to death as he would ever be while still breathing.

"How many of the agents are Reformationists?"

"Less than half . . . I don't know the exact number!" His eyes were rolled toward the thief master. "Most of them are out in the field, not here."

"How many in the temple? Their names?"

He started to name them, stammering, a few at first and then more, after several pauses, until he had called off a dozen in all. Barrett was one of them; Clay wondered if the man's body would ever be found.

"That's all . . . all I can remember. *Ahhhh!*"

Now Garlan's knife was touching him, moving to the most tender place. She twisted the blade, exerting pressure, Burrus never letting up on his own.

"If he lies, let him live—as less than a man!"

"Please, no!" He was begging Stone now. "Please, I've told you the truth. What more do you want from me?"

Clay was sickened by this deed as the man continued to blubber, pleading for mercy. He started to turn away, but Stone had more questions.

"How many on the space station, Worrel?"

There were fewer names this time, no more than a few of the hundred manning the station. Most of the station complement were technicians, and of those named Clay recognized only two as coming from that rank. One of them, however, was the medic who had given him the final check before releasing him to the surface.

Stone was satisfied. "I think he is telling the truth, Clay. Lacking the probe, though, there's only one way to test his story."

Burrus grunted. "You are finished with this one?"

"Not yet. Worrel, what signal do you have to warn each other of danger, and what will signal the attack on the native population?"

Worrel gasped again, once more feeling pressure from both blades. "The signal is 'Come First!' As to the attack, word is expected on the next ship from Earth."

Stone was startled. "Due within hours!"

"Yes—*aggghhhh!* Please, Stone, make them stop!"

"What means?"

"A plague strain, distributed into the water supplies of the various districts. It will generate itself once in human hosts. The Reformationists have been immunized against it."

"Where is the agent?"

"Already distributed to the various districts, but I don't know who in each area has charge—I *don't!* I'm not assigned to that part. Maybe the medic—I named him, didn't I?"

"It makes sense." Stone looked at Clay, nodding. "A viral reagent, and there's no better place to store biologicals than with other biologicals. The medic is almost always the only one to know what he carries in his kit."

He looked back to the hapless captive. "All right, Worrel,

you're going on ice. You should be thankful to be alive—you won't be, if we find that you have in any way lied."

"I haven't, Stone! So help me!"

"We are . . . even though it's more than you people seem willing to do for the Karyllians."

He sighed, turning away, and even in the darkness Clay could measure the burden of guilt weighing him down. Burrus let his eyes flick from the captive to Stone.

"Now you're through?" he asked.

"Yes."

"Good!" Burrus pressed his point farther, the razor-sharp obsidian slicing through cartilage, arteries, and veins alike. The blood spurted freely, the dead man giving a final gurgle as the last air trapped in his lungs escaped through the new opening in his windpipe. Before the convulsive final shudder was through, the natives holding the corpse let it drop, the half-severed head hitting the cobblestones like an overripe melon.

"Was that necessary?" demanded Stone, horrified.

The only answer to come from Burrus was another grunt, contemptuous. He turned toward the mouth of the alley, the temple visible only a short distance beyond.

Now they had to enter it.

SIXTEEN

As David Holland returned to the barracks with his fellow drones he carried his wife's final words, a warning that it would not be safe for them to meet again until Nathan made the arrangements for them to leave Earth. For now, the safest place for him was in the barracks.

"And you?" he asked.

"I'm staying in a rose tower." She smiled. "It's like being young again, David. I'd forgotten the inconveniences and adjustments you have to make. But I'm doing all right for a spoiled old rich lady."

Nathan was there as well, new ID covering most of the staff; he was the only one who found it necessary to travel. When David asked for the same, he was told that his face was too well known, thanks to the trial, which had concentrated on him almost to the exclusion of his tools. There wasn't time to arrange a facial restructuring, and if he was spotted by a citizen it would double the difficulties for everyone.

"Besides," said Nathan, "there are worse punishments than the barracks, David."

"I can't imagine them."

"The Jovian moons, for one. No man has survived a seven-year sentence in the mines. Their minds go first, and they almost always suicide."

"I've considered the idea," said Holland.

"Don't. Your life is not over. Whichever side wins on Karyllia, the Guided Worlds policy is as dead as the Compact. There's work for you there—why, man, there's need for a thousand projects!"

"And if the Reformationists win?"

"Then there are the colonies. A man with your qualifications would be welcomed anywhere, even if you were a multiple ax murderer."

And so he settled into the routine of barracks life, each day exactly like that which had preceded, a foretaste of that to follow. There were the booktapes, although he had never developed the habit of reading as an end in itself, for no other reason than pleasure. There were also men intelligent enough to stimulate the conversations, although he found out soon enough that their life experiences were so different there were almost no common meeting grounds. It was as though they spoke separate languages.

In one way the routine was beneficial as he adjusted to a regular schedule, rising each day at a certain hour, eating at regular times, retiring each night at the same moment. Janice had always made sure that his meals were balanced, that all essentials were included; but now mealtime became an event of inportance, each a break in the monotony. The food was always basic ration, unimaginatively prepared, but he managed to savor the most commonplace tastes, finding in each a depth of experience that required exploration. He *had* to explore; it helped consume a few more of the gray minutes.

There were other sweeps, the Firsters stepping up the level of their activity as the government's position became shakier; soon they would be able to force the new election that they wanted. But David was told to stay behind, lest one of his former antagonists spot his presence.

None of the activity spilled over onto the public channel, which varied not a bit in its bloody activities. On Nathan's next visit David asked why.

"Because the technicians control the programming for the public channel," was the reply. "We want to keep the drones in control, not hype them up to where they march against the government. It is possible to stampede even sheep with the proper stimulus, David."

"Why this constant exposure to violence?" he shuddered as
Doc Arko sliced up another nubile young female.

"A safety valve. A psychometrician could give you the tech-
nical words, but surrogate violence releases sexual tension and
stems the growth of emotional overcharges."

"But what is to prevent them from acting out what they
have seen?"

"Nothing, I suppose. It just doesn't work that way. The re-
pressed personality, the true ax-murderer type, is the one who
has no such outlet. Since the drones are under what amounts to
a lifetime of repression, they are given a strong dose in their entertainments."

Sex was another matter that was carefully regulated, scheduled weekly. Held under the cover of a social meeting, David
went along with the 80 per cent of his ward mates who lined
up eagerly at the blue warder's announcement to be ready. The
fifty or sixty who opted against socializing were far gone in
their narcotic fantasies as they suckled their joy juice bottles.

They were marched to one of the female wards on this same
level, where more than half of the men immediately paired off
with women who were obviously old weekly friends. There was
music, and the dining tables were lined with the sort of snacks
Holland remembered from childhood picnics; but few of the
visitors were interested in food at that point. Almost immediately the dormitory was in use.

Holland wandered for most of the three hours of the meeting, finding that sitting was an invitation to an approach from
one of the unpaired women. A few of them were pleasant
enough to look upon, but they were placid, even bovine. After
a lifetime with Janice he found them as dreary as the rest of
the drone existence.

It was a relief to escape back to his own ward when the signal came, even though most of his fellows seemed more than
self-satisfied. He never went again.

The routine became familiar, became a way of life that was
almost normal as the days slid into weeks, and even the weeks
slid by with a crashing sameness. He lost track of the date very

quickly, forced to ask Nathan on his rare visits. Each time he asked also if there was news from Karyllia, and each time the technician shook his head.

It was a deadening existence for a man whose entire life had been his work. Holland had never even thought about the four-hour or six-hour work period that was normal for most of the world. He spent as much time as necessary at his tasks, relaxing briefly only while making the necessary adjustment to a new problem. For him and Janice, socializing had been almost entirely political, their only friends the people working on the Project, or hangovers from early life such as Letermeister and a handful of others. He could not play games; there was no challenge in defeating someone else in a contest that had no meaning in real life.

In short, he had never been so bored in his life.

The weeks became a month, and then a second, and he missed Janice with a pain that was growing almost unbearable. He found himself watching the programming on the public channel not with interest, but at least as something to distract his mind; he even began to plan ways for Doc Arko to improve his record of carnage . . .

Nathan came one evening, seeming unusually harried; his eyes kept glancing nervously from face to face, even to the screen.

"We've unleashed the hurricane, David, and it does not seem that it can be brought under control. Even Wiley and his people are scared—the Firsters are almost completely out of hand. It may be that we'll have to cut off space flight for a few years."

"Why?"

"To stop the Firsters from taking over the ships and sending nukes to the star worlds."

"What about our own people?"

"There will be no problem with Karyllia and Locane, the men and women we have there can adapt nicely. The colonies will not have so easy a time of it. They depend on Earth, although we're studying now to see if we can support them from Karyllia."

He slumped in a chair, utterly weary, running a hand through already rumpled hair. For a moment his eyes closed, his features lined with pain. When he opened them again it was to blink, as though in his exhaustion he had forgotten where he was.

"We don't have much time, David—a week; perhaps even less. All starships will be dispatched from Prime Station as soon as the technicians' council has the data to permit a final decision. We're going to have to move you and Janice to Prime Station—probably within the next twenty-four hours. I may not be the one to come for you, so be ready for whatever happens."

"Have you heard from Karyllia?" he demanded.

"Yes . . ."

SEVENTEEN

The thieves went first, Clay and Stone holding back as the others infiltrated the temple, signaling to those of the guild who had preceded them earlier. The two agents stayed in the shadows along the walls, moving in the direction of the kitchen with Burrus. There was only one white robe in the area, lounging against the wall in apparent disinterest although his eyes continually flicked toward the entrance. After a moment he straightened, started casually in that direction as Stone touched Clay's arm to signal that the man was one of those named by Worrel.

Suddenly Garlan came darting from the side, brushing past the white-robed priest just as he reached the entrance, glancing off his side. Startled, the man cursed, turning to scream at her . . . as three of the thieves came from behind to strike at the same instant, their soul-blades drinking vital blood. They caught him before he could fall and carried him to the darkest corner, covering him with a native robe as curious eyes followed them briefly, then quickly became disinterested. In no more than ten seconds the dead man was one among scores of other sleepers.

"It's going too easily," Stone muttered, almost to himself. "I don't like it."

"They're asleep," said Clay.

"They shouldn't be."

They moved into the corridor that circled through the walls of the building, Garlan slipping off her own outer robe to become once more a servitor. Clay found his cell. He ducked in to find his belongings, which he had stored on the shelf beneath the bed when he left on his trip with Martin. He quickly changed, becoming once more one of the servants to the white robes, pulling the cowl over his head. He saw Stone slip grenades from each heel and did the same.

They slipped back into the corridor, only the three of them now; Burrus and the others were waiting in the main temple, the guild leader with Martin's communicator already tuned. At a signal from Stone or Clay they would invade the lower regions in full force.

Clay saw a white robe round the turn of the passageway and stiffened; but there was no signal from Stone, the man nodding at the agent-in-charge as he passed. Still the youth's spine was crawling with the anticipation of a strike from unexpected quarters.

A moment later they were descending, following the twists and turns designed to confuse, both Clay and Stone now wishing that the precautions had been simpler. Several of the passages doubled back upon themselves, while others became cul-de-sacs unexpectedly. Stone hoped Burrus could remember the detailed instructions he had given.

Another priest turned a corner, coming toward them with furrowed brow. He glanced at Stone without a word—then recognized Clay even with the cowl over his head. Startled, he stopped.

"Holland! I didn't know you were due back. Where is Martin?"

"In his cell," said Clay, hoping that his voice sounded casual. "He twisted his ankle; I'm going to send the medic to him now."

The explanation was accepted, although the lines remained in the man's face. He started past them with a nod, Stone turning to the side to give him room—and bringing his hand against the base of the man's skull in a chop that sent him sprawling. Immediately Garlan was upon him, her knife ready to slice across his throat . . . until Stone caught her, pulled her away.

"No more murders!" he said. "Only if we are attacked . . . and only if there is no other way!"

Contempt showed in her eyes as she stood and replaced her blade, but she said nothing as Clay first checked the nearest side room and then helped Stone drag the unconscious man inside. They emptied his heel caches, then checked him for other weapons, Stone removing his belt as well. Clay found a broad-bladed knife taped to his side, the blade nearly thirty centimeters long; it would stand well against a native sword. The knife was not standard issue, Stone hissing between his teeth as he saw it. Then he shook his head.

"I still think of the Compact even though I know it is dead, Clay. It's hard to change a life's orientation."

There were more than twenty agents in the temple; Worrel had named only a few of them as enemy. As they tied their captive's hands and applied pressure to the nervous system to ensure his continued sleep, Clay hoped that Worrel had not withheld the truth.

"Stay here, both of you," said Stone. "I'll check ahead, see what we're up against."

He was back a moment later, shaking his head. "There's half a dozen of them in the lounge—along with ten or so of the others. I can't call Burrus down to invade in force—he'll only slice the throats of the innocent as well as the Reformationists. We've got to get them out into the open, separate them."

Almost before Stone finished, Clay activated his communicator, spoke low: "Come First—the temple! Martin—"

He cut the phrase off without completing it, Stone startled, Garlan watching in idle curiosity as Clay's throat worked to subvocalize the warning. She could not hear the words, but the effect was almost immediate. Stone moved into the corridor to meet a number of white robes hurrying toward the stairs. They were followed by others, attracted by the call although presumably not understanding it.

Stone caught one of those by the arm, the man twisting with surprise. "Go back. Find Heath, Salyer, Merritt. Find out where they are, what they're doing, then come back here and tell me."

They spoke quietly as six of the named Reformationists moved past, several of them glancing suspiciously at Stone. But none of them stopped, responding to the urgent summons, several of them actually running now.

Stone stopped three or four more of the merely curious, sending them back; then he held up his hands to prevent a sudden surge of traffic.

"Go back, all of you. It's all right. Something is going to happen, but I want all of you to stay right here, out of the way."

Most of the agents did as he said, but as Clay came out of the side room Stone saw two of them sidling away, moving beyond the gathering room. They were deliberately not looking back as the man he had dispatched on the errand quickly returned.

"Heath is on duty in communications," said the man. I think Salyer is with him, but nobody knows where Merritt is."

Clay remembered the other agent who had been on the waterfront; perhaps that had been Merritt. If so, it was easy to guess that he would never again be seen in the temple.

Stone nodded as he accepted the information, keying his own communicator: "Burrus, there are six. Take them and come."

There were more curious glances as his message was heard by every agent there, but the last of the agents were returning to the gathering room, and now he moved after them, standing in the doorway.

"There is trouble, but I want every man here to stay here. If anyone tries to leave the room, the rest of you sit on him—do whatever you have to do to keep him here. I don't care if it's three men or ten men—the rest of you take them!"

He shut off the sudden questions by turning and leaving. "Clay! Those two—which way did they go?"

Clay was already trailing the two who had tried to slip away; now he turned a corner, saw them running. One looked back, flung a grenade—an explosive. The shattering sound was deafening in the stone corridor, chips flying and dust filling the air to make them choke and cough.

"They're going up!" said Stone, sweeping his hand through the air before him as though that would clear the dust. "To communications—this way!"

Clay and Garlan crowded on his heels as Stone pushed through the near bedlam in the gathering room to his office, where he swept aside a hanging to reveal a flight of stairs leading up. Without bothering to explain, he plunged up them, the other two hurrying after him. The rock dust had them gasping before they had gone halfway, but still Stone pushed on, until he came out on one of the upper levels.

The noise of the explosion had not penetrated, but now a few other agents were coming out of side rooms, aroused by what was happening. Stone stopped for no more than a second to get his bearings, then was moving again—and rounded a corner to come out at the head of another stairs where the two men were just pounding up.

They stopped, shocked to see Stone before them. The one who had thrown the first grenade made ready to do so again—and then he was shuddering, Garlan's soul-blade quivering in his throat, the point penetrating through the back of his neck. He scrabbled wildly at nothing, the grenade falling from his fingers to roll back down the stairs; and then he was falling with it, the explosion coming seconds later.

Garlan rushed toward the stairs, but Clay grabbed her, held her back.

"My soul!" she protested.

"Later! If it's whole you can reclaim it once this is done. If it's broken, it was in honor!"

The other man stared back in horror for an instant, then went to his knee to bring out a grenade of his own—from his left heel.

"You fool!" cried Stone. "You'll die with us!"

The man looked at the gas capsule in his fingers, shuddered once. Panicked, he looked back again; but the stairs were filled

with a roiling cloud of dust. The grenade went into his robe—
and one of the broad-bladed knives came out even as he rushed
forward.

Clay was moving almost without thinking, bringing out the
same knife he had taken from their first captive. He met the
rush by countering the sweeping stroke, steel clanging against
steel—and then he was bowled backward by the other's weight,
falling heavily to the floor. Clay's head cracked against the
stone, bringing stars, but he had managed to wrap his arms
about the other, trapping his upper arms and preventing him
from striking with his own blade. They started to roll, but before anything more could happen Garlan rushed forward and
delivered a sharp kick to the temple of the man, and when he
tried to twist away, another that broke the bridge of his nose.

Screaming with pain, the man's knife clattered from his
fingers as he grabbed at his face. Before Stone could interfere
Garlan had scooped it up to slash once across the throat, the
blood spurting across Clay.

The unbalanced weight of the dead man fell from Clay, leaving him stunned for an instant. Then Stone was grabbing his
hand, helping him up . . . just as the medic came staggering
out of his clinic, bowed down by two small cylinders made
heavy by their protective cases. He glanced toward Stone and
immediately turned in the opposite direction . . .

. . . to run into Burrus as the thief master rounded the
corner. The medic grunted as he slammed into the solid body
of the thief, then tried to twist past him. But Stone was already
calling out.

"Take him, Burrus—alive!"

It was too late for the last word; the knife was already spilling blood to add yet another stain to the bleached floor. One
cylinder clattered on the floor, Clay going stiff with fear; but
the case was strong enough to hold without damage as Burrus
stooped to wipe his blade clean.

"The six?" asked Stone.

"All dead," the thief replied.

Clay saw the revulsion in Peter Stone's eyes at the bloodthirst that dominated the natives. But there was no time to protest their violence. The agent gave one word and the others followed him back to the stairs, where the dust was at last settling. There they started up again, another flight, to the communications center.

The door was one of the few wooden panels in the place, the others being on the medic's clinic and the armory. Stone motioned the others back and brought out another grenade. The explosion shattered the native wood into splinters, the agent kicking through the debris before his ears had stopped ringing —to see one of the two men in the room frantically trying to raise the space station, just now moving out of radio darkness.

"Yes, Ahd-Abbor Prime, we read you." The voice was unemotional. "What is the problem?"

Burrus, Clay, and Garlan had knives at ready as they advanced on the two men, but there was no fight left in them. One stood, moving out of Stone's way as the agent took his place.

"This is Stone. Let me have Captain Lecastre." The station was nominally under naval command, although the complement was only six men. A moment later the station commandant was speaking.

"Yes, Peter. This is Lecastre. Ops tells me there's some upset. What is it?"

"Are you on the bridge? If so, go to the com and clear and lock. This is for your ears only."

"Moving now."

Nearly a moment passed; then the captain spoke again. "Yes, Peter. What is the mystery?"

"Come First!" said Stone, anxiously.

"I beg your pardon? Repeat, please."

He did, with the same confused response as at first. "That means nothing to you?"

"Nothing, Peter. Sorry."

"Good!" He proceeded to outline what had happened, ending with the list of names forced from Worrel. "I want those men arrested, I want every other man probed. I don't know how many others may be Reformationist sympathizers."

"None of mine, I'll wager," said Lecastre. "They'd never have made it past psychoprobing. Very well, Peter. What else?"

"The communicator is to go under your personal lock after you send one message to the field posts. All agents are to report to Ahd-Abbor immediately—those closer to a drop point should go there for pickup first. Has the ship from Earth arrived?"

"Not yet. We expect her momentarily."

"When she docks, use the naval forces to probe everyone on her. As soon as you have cleared enough of your own people, I want a shuttle and a probe here. You've got about six hours of darkness yet. Have the shuttle land on the temple roof."

Lecastre seemed shocked. "Against the Compact?"

Stone closed his eyes, tired. "Haven't you been listening? We're fighting to save the natives of this planet. The Compact is dead!"

"Very well, Peter. But I will have to make a full report to Earth, so I sincerely trust that you do know what you are doing."

He signed off, leaving Stone to sigh as he turned the unit to the personal range, then spoke again.

"This is Stone. All agents not in the lounge report there now. Repeat, now. There are natives in the restricted areas. Ignore them."

Ten minutes later he faced them; none had been restrained during the fighting. He explained briefly what had happened, what would happen.

"As soon as possible you'll be cleared and released to duty."

"What duty?" asked one. "If the Compact is no more, then what will we do here?"

"I don't know," said Stone. "I hope to have answers soon. For now, carry on as you have been."

The shuttle landed two hours before dawn, bringing the probe and an emissary from the technicians' council on Earth. There were no natives on the temple roof when the little ship touched down without lights, but Clay was sure that the roof-tops of the surrounding houses were well populated with Burrus' thieves, if no one else.

The probe quickly cleared most of the agents in the temple, although a few were found to be ripe for conversion to the Reformationist cause. The captives were put aboard the shuttle for transport back to the space station, where they would be placed under arrest and in detention. The others were reassembled and given a full explanation of what the Reformationists had planned.

There was shocked disbelief. "They'd have killed us as well?" demanded someone.

"If they hold no respect for the Karyllians, how can they respect their own kind?"

The emissary filled Stone in on the developments on Earth. As the man told of the arrest and farcical trial of the Hollands, Stone glanced quickly at Clay.

"It looks as though your population of Terrans is going to take a sudden jump, Stone. Do you have a place to put them?"

"It's too early to integrate them into Karyllian life," said Stone. "The mountain valleys will do, I suppose. The natives already avoid the area, call it the place of the devil-wizards. We'll have to set up a protected perimeter, to avoid even accidental contact. We may as well play the wizard role to the hilt."

"Always roles," said Clay. "Why can't we come out into the open, be what we are?"

"In time," said Stone. "Perhaps we won't be trying to secretly force the development of this planet, Clay, but we can't just throw them into Earth's technological era without some protection against cultural shock. Rub their noses in our superiority and we'll kill them just as surely as the Reformationists had planned. There's historical precedent to show what happens when disparate cultures meet and clash. The less advanced always wither and die."

"I must return," said the emissary. "I'll carry your recommendations to Earth, Stone. I don't think I'll be back."

He clasped hands with Stone and nodded to Clay, and was gone with the shuttle, departing just before the first light touched the east. The two men made their weary way back down into the temple, coming upon Garlan rolled up in a corner of the corridor. She had regained her soul-blade, unbroken, and clutched it now as she slept soundly, her dress marked with the scars of battle.

Clay gazed upon her for a moment, his emotions confused; he moved quietly past, so as not to wake her.

Then they were in Stone's office, slumping in their chairs, ready to surrender to the need for sleep. But one question yet demanded explanation.

"Tell me," Clay insisted. "Why did they call me android?"

Stone sighed, and began to explain . . .

EIGHTEEN

The naval forces of Earth arrived in Karyllian space in ones and twos, and then in larger numbers, until there were more than fifty. Some entered permanent parking orbits, while others were merely establishing a new base for contact with Locane and the colonies, and for the probes that would continue to search for new systems and new worlds hospitable to man.

None would go back to Earth until word came from the single starship left hidden where only the technicians could find it that the planet had returned to normal.

The agents scattered over the planet had been returning to Ahd-Abbor in slow numbers, taken and probed; most of them were found to be sympathetic to the Reformationists. The suggestion was made that they be returned to Earth, but the ships' crews declined to provide passage. And so they were sent into the mountains to work alongside the new arrivals. Unlike the rest of Earth's exiles, however, they were forbidden contact with the Karyllians under any guise.

David and Janice Holland arrived on one of the first ships, to be greeted by Clay. During the weeks of waiting for them he had been plagued by doubts as to the way he should react to them. But when he saw them at last and was welcomed with his father's clasped arms and his mother's embrace, he knew that biological origins meant nothing. They were his parents; they had overseen his birth, had given him creation even if not a part of their own life-force. Android or not, he was their son.

Earth was completely cut off from the stars now, the Bad Years already begun. But the next revolution was already in the planning, and while the stars winked once and looked again, it would be done . . .